Death
on the
Night
Watch

A Reverend Rob Vander Laan Mystery

Terry Hager

Acknowledgements

Thanks to all who gave me valuable feedback, criticism and specific input: Pat Allen, Dick Bewell, Tom Brink, Bill Decker, Bud Ipema, Lucinda Grover, Paul Haase, Al Helder, Mary Ippel, Tom Ippel, Tim Limburg, Pablo Martinez, Ron Norton, Bill Stroo, Jim Ulrey, Daryl Vander Kooi, Jim Vander Schaaf, Jonas Weisel, George Zuiderveen. Thanks to all other family and friends who stood by me through the long process of learning to write my first mystery.

Thanks to Lori Vanden Bosch and Deni Dietz for their copy-editing skills.

And a special thanks to my wife, Ruth, for all her readings, for her insightful criticisms and for always being there for me.

This Book is dedicated to the Reverend John Allen, 1937-1971, Founding Director of the Grand Rapids Youth Ministry. His passion for the alienated still inspires me.

CHAPTER I

I stood frozen at the entrance to the gang's apartment, my gaze riveted on the body of the girl across the room. Weak light from an old standing lamp in the living room fell on her where she lay sprawled in the kitchen doorway. She wore the gang colors—denim vest with the gang's name on the back: Lost Souls. The only sound I heard was the hammering in my chest.

When I'd graduated from seminary the previous year—1968, at age 33—and taken the job at the Street Ministry, I hadn't, in my wildest imaginings, anticipated something like this.

I gave myself a mental shake and hurried forward. The girl's head was turned to the side, toward the light. Now I could see it was Star. Dark splotches stained the back of her vest, and drying blood spread over the cracked linoleum floor. I smelled an odor I couldn't identify but would never forget.

Stomach in my throat, I lurched to the kitchen sink, stepping around the crimson pools and Star's body. I thought I would vomit, but the nausea decreased. My legs felt rubbery and the room spun. I staggered to a chair by the table, sank into it, and hung my head between my knees.

A moment later, no longer dizzy, I stepped over to Star's

body and touched her neck. No pulse. Still, I should have checked right away.

A couple of weeks earlier, she'd confided in me that she joined the gang because it was safer than living at home. Despite my probing, she'd refused to elaborate. The hurt in her eyes had touched me deeply.

"Oh God, why Star?" I groaned.

I knew the gang had no phone. I turned to make my way out of the apartment as a door squeaked behind me. I spun around, my heart threatening to burst from my chest. Mad Dog, one of the gang members stared at me from the closet. Blond crew cut, scar from his right ear down his cheek, he was all muscle. He wore no shirt under his colors.

"Rob?" he said.

"Mad Dog," I said, my voice pitched an octave higher than normal. "What the heck are you doing in the closet? What happened?"

He pushed the door open all the way, stepped out, and dropped into the chair I'd sat in a moment earlier, a look of panic in his eyes. Sweat dripped from his face. "I just found her there. I heard you come in, and I thought maybe it was whoever done this comin' back, so I hid in there." He jerked a thumb toward the closet. "Then you said somethin' and I could tell it was you."

"Come on," I said, putting a hand on his shoulder. "We have to get someone to call the police. Watch out for the blood."

We hurried to the front apartment where the voice of a popular TV talk show host and the laughter of the audience intruded into the hallway. I had to knock several times before an old man in a dirty undershirt and baggy pants opened the door a crack, the chain on the night lock preventing an unwelcome entry. I asked him to call the police and report the murder.

Still nauseated, I collapsed to the hallway floor and

waited for the cops to make the scene. Mad Dog slid down next to me.

I glanced up at the burned-out overhead bulb in the darkened hallway. The only dead bodies I'd seen before had lain peacefully in their caskets. Except for pretend murder victims on my favorite cop shows. But this was real. The blood. The smell. Someone I knew.

The sound of sirens winding down forced their way through the fog in my brain. A moment later four uniformed cops came cautiously through the front door of the building, hands resting on their holstered guns. One shined a flashlight in my face, blinding me. I covered my eyes with my hand. The light moved to Mad Dog and back to me.

The officer must have noticed my clerical collar. "You the priest who found the body?"

I rose to my feet, nodding, not bothering to tell him I was a minister, not a priest. Mad Dog stood up when I did. I kept my eyes shielded until the officer lowered the light.

"She's in there." I pointed toward the open door at the far end of the hallway. The officer aimed the beam in that direction.

"Anybody in the apartment besides the dead girl?"

I shook my head, then looked at Mad Dog. "I don't think so."

"Who called it in for you?"

I pointed at the old man from the front apartment, now standing behind the police.

The officer glanced back, then returned his attention to me. "What's your name?"

"Robert Vander Laan."

"Uh-huh," said the cop with a that-explains-it look on his face. "You're with that Street Ministry place downtown."

"Yes."

The light shifted to Mad Dog. "And who are you?"

"Ernie Larkin."

"Turn around, Mr. Larkin."

Mad Dog turned around. The flashlight illuminated his colors.

"Uh-huh," said the cop in the same tone he'd used with me. He motioned for Mad Dog to face him. "Know who the dead girl is, Mr. Larkin?"

"Star."

The officer looked at me, and I said, "She's a member of the gang."

"Was Mr. Larkin with you when you discovered the body?"

I hesitated, glancing at Mad Dog. "He was in the closet. When he realized it was me in the room, he came out."

The cop turned to one of the other uniforms. "Take these guys out on the porch and keep them there till the detectives can talk to them." He gestured toward another officer. "Check with the guy who called it in."

The officer in charge moved down the hallway to the Souls' apartment, followed by his jowly-faced partner. They entered cautiously, guns drawn. Mad Dog and I moved outside and sat on one side of the wide front steps as an officer stationed himself behind us on the porch. Several minutes later, a middle-aged man in a dark suit with an I.D. badge on it arrived. He carried a medical bag and exchanged greetings with the officer at the door who called him "Doc."

Occasional laughter erupted from the Souls' apartment. What could be funny, I wondered, with Star's dead body lying a few feet away?

Two plainclothes officers pulled up, emerged from their car with a camera and a canvas bag, and entered the building. Another unmarked car pulled up with two more plainclothes cops. The cop with the jowly face came out to get something from his cruiser, and the two latest arrivals walked up the front sidewalk with him. One of them asked Jowly Face a question I didn't hear. He answered, "Yeah, she was stabbed multiple times."

I shuddered.

"Detective Johnson. Detective Kincaid," said the cop behind us, greeting the two plainclothes officers.

Detective Johnson was middle-aged with a florid face and a comb-over that could only have fooled a legally blind person. His belly pushed open his jacket. He ignored Mad Dog and me.

The younger detective, slight, with dark hair, glanced at me, then turned to the senior detective. "Do you want me to interview—"

"Let's check the scene," the older detective growled. He looked at the cop by the door, jerking his thumb backward. "Put the gang scum bag in your car." The detectives disappeared inside.

The cop stationed at the door took Mad Dog by the arm and escorted him to one of the cruisers.

"Hang in there, Mad Dog," I called. "I'll check with you later."

After several minutes the detectives returned to the front porch. Johnson scowled at me. I rose to my feet so I wouldn't have to look up at him, and the smell of garlic almost knocked me over. I tried to imagine looking through his eyes as he gave me the once over. His gaze lingered first on my black wingtip shoes, then slowly rose up my stocky 5'9" frame, taking in my jeans, clerical shirt, longish brown hair, full beard and blue eyes.

"You're Vander Laan. You the one who found the dead girl?"

"Yes, I found Star."

The other detective pulled out a notebook and pen from the inside pocket of his sport jacket.

Johnson took a step closer, too close for my comfort level. "What were you doing here?" he demanded

"I work with the Street Ministry. The gang invited me to stop over." I didn't tell him they wanted to discuss the police crackdown on them.

"Street Ministry," he repeated with a note of contempt. "You're talking about that hangout for lowlifes on Jefferson?"

"We're located on Jefferson, yes." I kept my voice neutral, surprised at Johnson's intimidating tone. I knew the cops in Grand Rapids, Michigan, did not view the Street Ministry as an asset to the community. I couldn't blame them since my "congregation" included hippies, who used illegal drugs, and gang kids, who were sometimes arrested for things like assault and breaking and entering. Still, in previous encounters I'd had with the cops, I'd been treated civilly.

Johnson continued in the same aggressive tone. "What time did you find the body?"

"Just before midnight."

"And this Ernie character was in the apartment when you got there?"

"Yes. He was hiding in the closet. He scared the crap out of me when he came out." I repeated what Mad Dog had told me.

"So the dead girl's name is Star?"

"Her real name is Susan." Nicknames of downtown kids had seemed silly to me, until I came to understand the pain and alienation hidden under or flaunted by their new handles. "Her parents are Corey and Alice Wynsma."

"Know where the Wynsmas live?"

"No. Just met them recently at a church meeting."

"You touch anything in the apartment?"

"I don't know. Uh, I must have touched the counter by the sink when I felt like throwing up. Maybe the chair by the table. And the door knob, of course, when I came in."

"You always barge into the gang's place when no one answers the door?"

"The apartment was too quiet, and the gang expected

me. Plus, the door wasn't closed all the way, so I pushed it open. I saw the body lying in the kitchen doorway and went in to check."

Why was Johnson so overtly hostile? His name rang a bell, but I couldn't say why.

"That goofy-looking car parked at the curb yours?" He jerked a thumb toward the green sedan I'd bought new, just before graduating from seminary. I discovered too late that it looked exactly like the vice squad cars. Whenever I pulled into the lot where kids hung out, they would head for the hills until somebody yelled, "It's only Rob."

"Yes, it's my car," I said.

"You paint all that god-awful stuff on it so your punks could see you weren't Vice?"

"One of the downtown people did it for me."

When the young artist made me the offer, I'd assumed we'd be discussing what he'd paint on it, so I was surprised when I walked out of my office one day to find my car covered with a cross, a peace sign, a light house, flowers and the words NIGHT WATCH. Outrageous as it looked, I'd grown attached to it.

I'd asked the artist the significance of "NIGHT WATCH."

"It's what you do," he said. "You watch over us night people."

My car was now known as Night Watch in the downtown scene.

"What's going to happen to Ernie?" I asked the detective.

He ignored my question. "He surprised you coming out of that closet in the kitchen?"

"Right." I refrained from telling him I'd already answered that.

"How did he get along with the dead girl? Did he have a thing for her? Were they fighting?"

"I don't know. Star is, or was, the girlfriend of Red Feather, the vice president of the gang."

"Where were you before you came here?"

"At some bars on South Division." I gave him the names of the bartenders, who would confirm my presence. The bars were all frequent stops on my night ministry rounds.

Johnson turned to his partner. "Think we should take the Reverend to an interrogation room at the station for more questions, Kincaid?"

I had the feeling he wasn't serious, maybe trying to intimidate me or hassle his partner.

Detective Kincaid shuffled his feet. "A modicum of empathy might be apropos," he finally said. "Reverend Vander Laan looks disconcerted from discovering the victim." Then he hastened to add, "However, you'd know the wisest course."

Huh? Even in my freaked-out state, that sounded like a strange way for a cop to talk.

Johnson pulled his head back a fraction and scowled as he looked at his partner. Then he shrugged, asked for phone numbers where I could be reached, and told me to go to the police station for fingerprinting. I promised I'd be available to answer further questions.

I could hardly wait for another conversation with this representative of Grand Rapids's finest.

Still in a daze, I left the apartment building and drove to the police station to get printed. I wanted to go straight home afterwards but decided to swing by the Street Ministry building. In addition to housing our offices, it was the location of Drop-in, the "hangout for lowlifes," according to Johnson. Normally it closed at midnight. The lights were on, however, and two police cars were parked in front of the building. As I walked toward the entrance, I saw Red Feather, the vice president of the gang, in the back seat of one of the squad cars. He glanced at me, a haunted look in his eyes. I was glad now that we'd arranged for an attorney on our board to do a session for the kids on their Miranda rights.

I climbed the steps at the front of the dark green two-story house that had been remodeled sometime in the past to serve as office space. A volunteer sat at the reception desk. The desk, like all the furniture in the building, was a hand-me-down from one of the many Grand Rapids furniture manufacturers. The volunteer's right heel tapped rapidly against the floor. "Did you hear about Star?"

"Just came from the Souls' pad." I looked toward Drop-in, comprised of the room to the left of the reception area and the one behind it. A large archway connected the rooms so that the space functioned as one open area.

Some heavies—gang members—and a few other Drop-in regulars sat around a low table. Other heavies stood around the room or sat on chairs and pillows along the wall with a half dozen hippies—heads, in the downtown jargon. The two groups got along surprisingly well, perhaps sensing a bond in their alienation from mainstream culture. Nathan leaned against a wall in the corner. Twenty-one, shoulder-length red hair and long sideburns, he handled the job of Drop-in coordinator with brilliance and humor. Volunteers were scattered among the kids. It was their job to listen and counsel the kids and to prevent fights and illegal activities on the premises. Everyone looked shaken. Two uniformed police officers standing near the arch turned to look at me as I entered. I nodded to them and then slid on to an empty chair at the table.

Red Feather entered the room and dropped into the chair next to mine. He ran his fingers through long, dark hair that hung down his back. "You been at the pad?" he asked.

"Yes," I answered. "The cops questioned me there. What happened?"

Red Feather let out a deep sigh. "We was all hanging out in the park, except for Star and Mad Dog and Outlaw." Outlaw was the gang's president.

"Where was Mad Dog?"

Red Feather shrugged.

One of the uniformed officers edged closer. Red Feather glanced at him, then looked at the floor.

"It's okay," I said. "Go on."

"When it got close to time for our meeting with you," Red Feather said, looking up, "we headed over to the pad. That's when we found Star." He held his breath for a moment, probably to keep his emotions from spilling out. "We hightailed it out of there, but I talked everybody into comin' here. We musta left just before you got there."

Nathan moved to a small table in the corner. He picked up the coffee pot and filled a cup. "They told me about finding Star's body, so I called the cops and said the gang would wait for them here. The cops should be just about finished."

Someone called from outside and the two cops left the room.

I turned to Cat, a tall, buxom redhead, Outlaw's girl. "Where's Outlaw?"

"He got pissed tonight and took off on his motorcycle."

I hoped Outlaw had a good alibi.

CHAPTER 2

My mind buzzed with more questions I wanted to ask the gang members. "Nathan," I said, "any chance you could spend the night so the gang can crash here? They won't be able to go back to the apartment."

"No problem."

A few minutes later, we closed the building to all but the gang. As things settled down, I said, "When did you guys last see Star alive?"

She was in the parking lot with us about nine," said Cat. "She said she was coming here to use the john."

"Nobody saw her after that?"

Some kids shook their heads, others shrugged.

"Did she show up here, Nathan? I said.

"Nobody saw her."

"And nobody knows where Outlaw is?"

More head-shaking and shrugging.

"Where the hell is Mad Dog?" asked Red Feather.

I told them about Mad Dog's nearly giving me a heart attack at the apartment and that I'd last seen him in the cruiser, waiting to be interrogated. "They may have taken him to the station for questioning."

Red Feather sat with his arms resting on his knees, head hanging down.

"I'm sorry about Star," I said, squeezing his shoulder.

A short time later, I drove home in a state of exhaustion. I didn't want to think about the murder. My mind drifted to the invitation I'd just received to serve as the pastor of Washington Avenue Church, a half dozen blocks from where I lived. The church neighborhood used to be populated largely by offspring of Dutch immigrants who had settled in West Michigan after the mid-1800's. Recently black families had begun moving into the area, and the idea of serving in a church and neighborhood like that appealed to me. I'd only planned to be at the Street Ministry a couple of years anyway. Staying longer might give me a questionable reputation and decrease future ministry options within my conservative Dutch denomination.

The problem was I'd come to care about my congregation a lot more than I'd ever anticipated.

And now one of them, Star, had been murdered, her light snuffed out. I wanted to run away.

If I accepted the call to Washington Avenue, no one would know I was running away.

Except me.

And God.

When I got home I felt an urgent need to connect with Jackie. "Wake up, babe," I whispered, as I sat on the bed and shook her shoulder gently.

"Hey," she said. "What's up?" Her long blond hair was mussed, and her eyelids drooped over her green eyes.

"One of the kids was murdered tonight. I found the body."

She bolted upright. "Who?"

"Star." Jackie knew many of the kids from her occasional visits to Drop-in. "I never signed up for this," I hissed, trying to keep my voice down so as not to wake Andy, our five-year-old son. "She was only seventeen."

Jackie got up and put on a robe. "Why don't we go downstairs? I'll make some tea."

A short time later we sat on the couch in the living room. I told her about finding the body at the Souls' apartment, being questioned there, and talking with the kids at Drop-in. Then I said, "I only learned Star's real name a couple of weeks ago. It's Susan."

"How'd you find that out?"

"I met her parents at that presentation on my work at Woodhaven Church." I set my cup on the table and began pacing the room. "After my spiel, a couple introduced themselves as Corey and Alice Wynsma. We did the Dutch Bingo thing." I referred to the practice of checking into family connections Dutch-American folks often do upon meeting. Instead of someone calling out numbers, we mention names of people we are related to until, bingo, a connection between strangers is made through the larger Dutch-American community and a beginning trust is established "Alice told me that her daughter was hanging out downtown," I continued, "and that lately she was often gone from home for days at a time."

"Did her folks know her downtown nickname?"

"No. So I didn't realize we were talking about Star until Alice showed me a picture. With everything in the news about gangs and drugs, they were worried sick about her."

I sat down again. I couldn't seem to get enough air.

"Did you tell Star you talked with her parents?"

"Didn't have to. Star came into my office and said her folks told her. She got ticked off when I said her mom wanted me to keep an eye on her. She said it was none of her mom's business what she did downtown. I assured her I wouldn't be reporting to her mom." Something in my chest moved up to my throat, making it difficult to swallow.

"Did Star's parents know her boyfriend is part Cherokee and vice president of the gang?"

I resumed pacing. "I asked Star if her folks had met Red Feather. She didn't think they could handle it, but I told her not knowing him might be harder."

"Did she say she'd introduce him?"

My head began to ache. "Said she'd think about it."

"Her parents sound nice. Why do you think she joined the gang?

"I'm not certain. You know that some of the kids have been molested or abused in some way. Often they've been teased and bullied by their peers. Sometimes their parents have kicked them out, but that's not the case with Star. She told me recently it wasn't safe for her at home, but she wouldn't be more specific."

Jackie shook her head in a barely perceptible movement, but said nothing.

I rubbed my eyes as I paced. "Star looked like a kid who belonged in the front row of a church youth group, but she looked just as much at home with the gang. Oh, that reminds me." I reached into my pocket and withdrew a gold chain with a peace sign on it. The clasp was broken. "Star dropped this in my office. Interesting piece of jewelry for a gang member. Meant to give it back …" I clutched it tightly in my fist.

* * *

The next day I struggled to do some Ministry-related paperwork in my study at home, but my gaze kept shifting to the letter from Washington Avenue Church, which lay on my desk. I admired the church's commitment to stay in the city rather than move to the suburbs. As pastor at Washington Avenue, I'd be engaged in a more normal ministry. Of course, most in my denomination would hardly consider a ministry in a changing neighborhood like Washington Avenue "normal."

I thought about my parents. Dad never tried to influence me, but Mother made it abundantly clear that it was a huge mistake for me to have declined the call to the church in Iowa after I graduated from seminary. She wouldn't approve of a church like Washington Avenue, but she'd see it as a significant step up from the Street Ministry.

Elbows propped on my desk, head in my hands, I prayed for guidance. I saw Star's body lying on that cracked linoleum floor. I recalled that smell. How could I leave the Street Ministry before the police had solved this murder and the kids had gotten through some of their grief?

* * *

"She was such a likable kid," I said to Nathan.

We were in my Drop-in coordinator's office at the Ministry the evening after the murder. I knew that, like me, Nathan was particularly fond of Star.

"Star usually had a good word and a smile for everybody," I said.

Nathan sat on the corner of his desk. "She was pretty wild at first, drinking and fighting. Remember when she got into that knife fight with one of the girls? She really shaped up, though, after Red Feather fell for her."

"Lately she seemed to gravitate toward any kid that seemed upset."

Nathan smiled. "I told her we needed to find a spare clerical collar for her."

"Seen anything of Mad Dog?"

"Cat said the police released him after questioning him at the station. Think he did it?"

I shrugged. "I believed him at the apartment."

When Nathan's phone buzzed, he picked it up and said, "Yes?" When, he hung up he said, "Stu's here and wants to interview us about Star's murder. Want to go first? I need to talk with one of the new volunteers for a bit."

Stu Peterson, a reporter for the West Michigan Times, had done a couple of stories on the Street Ministry. Some of the kids were proud of their pictures and quotes in the paper.

Stu interviewed me in my office downstairs, next to Drop-In. When we were finished I rose from my chair to say good-bye. "I don't know if you're up for it, Rob," he said, "but I'd like to tag along with you tonight. See what else I can learn about the Street Ministry."

Looking at the prematurely bald and diminutive reporter, I thought about his request. Getting back to work was probably the best medicine for me, and I liked the idea of facing the night with the amiable Stu. "Sounds good." I said. "Give me a few minutes to make a call, and then we'll hit the streets."

"Don't hurry," he said. "I've got a few questions for Nathan."

I didn't want to be distracted, so I closed the picture window drapes. I'd put off calling Star's parents long enough. I looked up the number and dialed. Corey answered.

"Corey, I just wanted you to know how sorry I am …" I swallowed. "How sorry I am about Susan."

"Thanks, Rob." His voice sounded pinched. "Susan told us quite a bit about you and the Street Ministry, after we met you at our church. You were very important to her." He stifled a sob.

I cleared my throat. "How are you and Alice holding up?"

"We cling to our good memories of Susan, and we've got lots of support."

"I wonder if I could stop over for a few minutes in the

next couple of days. If it's too much of an imposition, just say so."

"Hold on. Let me check with Alice."

A moment later, Corey said, "How about tomorrow afternoon, say, around two?"

I hung up the phone and massaged my temples. I tried to imagine what it was like for Corey and Alice, what it would be like to lose my son Andy. I winced.

I looked at the framed photo on my desk. I remembered reading a story to my little towhead that evening as he sat on my lap, his finger following the words on the page. Maybe he was smaller than the average five-year-old, but he was definitely smarter. After prayers and a good night kiss, I'd stood outside his door for a moment to listen for any wheezing. Humid weather sometimes aggravated his asthma, but he sounded fine.

I picked up the photo and rubbed a thumb over Andy's image.

A buzz from my phone startled me. Nathan said, "Detective Johnson's here to see you, Rob."

The detective appeared at my office door before I had a chance to ask Nathan to show him in. I hung up the phone.

Johnson paused in the doorway long enough to say, "Interview the guy at the desk, Kincaid. Find out what he heard about the murder from the hoodlums who hang out here." Then he entered, closing the door behind him.

"Good evening, Detective Johnson," I said. "Welcome to the Street Ministry."

He ignored my greeting. The aroma of garlic preceded him. The evening breeze had rearranged his comb-over.

I came around and sat on the front of my desk.

"What do you know about this murder that you haven't told me, Vander Laan?"

"I don't know anything more than I told you last night."

"Right now, I'm thinking Outlaw or Ernie Larkin or both

of them look pretty good for the murder. What do you know about Outlaw?"

"You may find this hard to believe, Detective, but they're not bad—"

"Yeah, yeah, they're all good kids. I asked you what you know about Outlaw."

"You probably know he's president of the Lost Souls. Before that, he was president of the Night Stalkers." That gang had recently merged with the Souls. "I heard he was working for a circus when he first came to town. Not a lot more I can tell you."

"You see Outlaw last night?"

"No."

"Know where he was?"

"No."

"You didn't see him anywhere while you were out prowling the streets?"

"No."

"You talk to anyone who knows where he was?"

"No."

I stood up, and Johnson moved so close to me his belly pushed against my stomach. The smell of cigarette smoke and garlic was overpowering. I'd have stepped back if my butt weren't already pressed against my desk. "If you're holding out on me," he said, "I'll bust your ass so fast it'll make that white collar of yours spin."

"I'd appreciate it if you didn't stand so close, Detective."

Johnson grabbed my clerical shirt and pulled me to within inches of his nose. "I'll stand wherever the hell I please, Vander Laan. And before the year's over, I'll close this place down so these pansy-assed kiddies won't have a clergyman to hide behind."

He let go of my shirt and stepped back. I looked him in the eye and said, "God bless you, Johnson."

He stared back, red-faced. "Detective Johnson to you."

"And it's Reverend Vander Laan to you."

He stood with his fists balled and rocked on his feet. I wondered if he would hit me. He looked like he could barely contain his rage. At last he pivoted, opened the door, and stalked out. He slammed the door behind him.

Shaking, I sat down in the chair behind my desk. I wasn't sure whether it was rage or fear I felt. Or both.

Nathan stepped into my office a moment later. "Johnson just stormed out of the building. What happened?"

I told him about my exchange with the detective.

"You can't let him close us down," said Nathan.

"I know."

"You demanded he call you Reverend? You tell everybody not to do that."

I scowled. "In Johnson's case, I'll make an exception."

Nathan shook his head, flashed the peace sign, and left my office.

I'd met cops like Sid Johnson when I lived in Cicero, a suburb of Chicago. Another lifetime. I'd been in a few scrapes with the cops there and joined a fledging gang that never quite got off the ground. I always suspected that one of the reasons my dad took the call to the church in Holland, Michigan, was to get his wayward adolescent into a different environment.

Before I could cool off from my confrontation with Johnson, Blaine Hanson walked in. Short dark hair, full beard, he had penetrating brown eyes. Those eyes could make you feel like you were the only important person in his world. I stood to shake hands. Blaine took my hand in both of his. He'd resigned six months earlier as director of this off-beat inter-denominational ministry he'd established, and that's when I'd taken over the job. He now served on our board of directors.

"How are you doing with finding Star's body?" he asked as we both sat down.

"Still in shock," I said. "I don't like talking about it." A shudder went through me.

"Make yourself talk about it. I promise it will get easier."

"I'm glad you came. I want to ask you about the detective leading the investigation. He seems awfully hostile. Does the name Johnson mean anything to you?"

Blaine folded his hands, stared at them for so long that I began to suspect the answer must relate to the experience that eventually led to his leaving the Street Ministry.

I came around my desk, eased into the chair next to him and waited. I'd worked with Blaine for the better part of a year as he struggled to readjust to his job and his life after THE EVENT. He'd never talked about it, and I'd only gotten sketchy details from other staff.

At last his eyes met mine. He spoke so softly I could only hear him because I was sitting right next to him. "Johnson's son was the cop Zeke shot and got sent up for."

knows I'm there. Zeke's head jerks up. He yells for me to stay away. I ask him what the trouble is."

Sweat glistened on Blaine's forehead. He turned a chair around, propped a foot on it, and gripped the back of it with his hands. "Zeke says something like, 'I blew it, man, but the bastard didn't give me a choice. If he'd just given me the money. But, no, he had to be a tough guy.' So I move toward him, since I have him talking, and ask him to let me help him. He's really agitated. He tells me not to come any closer, that nobody can help him. I get really scared when he points the gun at himself and threatens to eat it.

"I take another step toward him and tell him not do that, tell him we can get through this. He points the gun at me again. I'm a couple of feet away now." Blaine's knuckles were white as he gripped the chair. "He says something like 'Doesn't matter anyway. My old man's right. I'm just a piece of garbage.' I tell him that's not true and remind him of that poem one of the kids wrote that's still on the wall in Drop-in, you know, the one titled God Don't Make Junk. Zeke quotes the whole damn poem and then lets out this god-awful sob."

Blaine took a moment to gather himself as a single tear rolled down his cheek. Another ragged breath. "I ask him to give me the gun before he hurts himself. He looks up at me like maybe he's ready to give it to me."

Blaine resumed pacing. "I move up to him and reach out my hand, willing him to give me the gun. That's when there's a shout from my right: 'Police. Drop the gun.' Zeke whips the gun toward the sound and shoots. Twice."

Blaine's words had begun to tumble out now as if he were eager to be done with the story. "I turn to see the cop falling slowly forward. 'Oh, Jesus,' Zeke says. Lets his gun fall to the ground. A moment later the cop's partner has Zeke in cuffs, and an ambulance is on the way. Too late for Officer Johnson."

Blaine slumped into the chair and wiped the back of his

hand across his forehead. "I can still see the look of loath-ing in the cop's eyes and hear the words he spat at me. 'Rex would have gotten this slime-ball if you hadn't been in the line of fire.'"

Blaine squared his shoulders and looked at me. "Rex was Detective Johnson's son, a rookie on the force." He smiled a smile that didn't blot out the pain in his eyes. "It's getting easier. Wanted to tell you about it for a long time."

I could only imagine the effort it took him to tell—and re-live—the event. I felt grateful, as if I'd been given a huge gift of trust. "Thanks," I said.

We sat quietly for a moment. "You asked about Detective Johnson," said Blaine, looking more relaxed now. "What do you think of his partner?"

I knew that Blaine and the police chief went to the same church, and sometimes socialized with their wives, despite the general negative feeling in the department toward the Street Ministry. That must be how he knew of Kincaid.

"The man puzzles me," I said. "He doesn't talk like I'd expect a cop to talk."

"His father teaches at U of M. English Literature. Chief says Kincaid's a fine cop, really smart, but other cops don't like him because of his fancy vocabulary. Please keep that confidential."

Blaine opened the drapes. I looked out the window and saw Brandon Sharpe step out of his Cadillac. He waved at Blaine and me as he headed toward the Ministry. Brandon had the camera store diagonally across the street, as well as a few other businesses. He also served on our board of directors.

I stood and Blaine and I embraced silently. He gripped both my shoulders and said, "Give a yell if you need to talk."

"Same goes for you."

He left my office and I heard him exchange greetings with Brandon. I sat behind my desk and gazed out the window, digesting the information Blaine had given me. What he had gone through, I realized, made me feel slightly better about finding Star's body. After a couple of minutes Brandon entered. I motioned him to take a seat.

Tall and thin, dressed in an expensive suit, he peered at me intently. He asked how I was coping. He peppered me with questions about finding Star's body and what the police were doing. I filled him in but did not tell him about my latest encounter with Detective Johnson.

"I have to run," he said finally. In the doorway he turned back. "Don't get so wrapped up in this that you forget about you. I've told you before, you can go as far as you want in your career. Don't let this mess you up."

I appreciated Brandon's support, but there were others I preferred to confide in. I was glad he'd spared me his self-made-man speech since I'd already heard it. Twice. Brandon seemed oblivious to the people who'd helped make him a success. To me, life was about connections, relationships.

I left the building a few minutes later with Stu Peterson. We boarded Night Watch to begin my rounds.

"I've got a good feel for what you guys do with kids that hang around Drop-in," said Stu, "but what you do away from the building is a mystery."

"It's pretty simple. I hit nightspots, bars mostly, around the city, chat with people, listen to their troubles, make some suggestions. Often I just show an interest in them without judging them. And my collar tells them I'm doing it for the church."

"Sort of like God's bartender."

I hoped Stu wouldn't use that for the theme of a story.

Sometimes I pondered the significance and legitimacy of my ministry and struggled to ground it theologically in my sober Reformed tradition. On the one hand, I thought the notion of God's bartender sounded perfect. On the other hand, it was way too light-hearted to be theologically sound.

This was certainly no time to wrestle with that. Preoccupied with Star's death, I could barely muster up energy to go through the motions of my job. Part of me felt like doing business as usual diminished her death. Yet, that's what I had to do.

"Isn't the apartment where you found Star's body near here?" asked Stu.

"You haven't been there?"

"No. One of our photographers went over, but I didn't go."

I took a right at the next corner, then a left and parked. I pointed at a once elegant, now dilapidated Victorian house, wondering what secrets it might reveal if only it could talk. Most of all, I wished it could tell us who murdered Susan Wynsma.

"Think one of the gang members did it?" said Stu.

"It's possible, but I can't wrap my mind around that. If it wasn't one of the gang kids, I haven't the foggiest who killed her."

"Another kid who hangs around your place, maybe, who isn't in the gang?"

I thought of Arnold, a guy in the downtown scene I hardly knew, a guy the other kids tried to avoid. I shrugged and said, "My job is to deal with the effects of Star's murder on the rest of the downtown people. I wish the cops luck."

So why did I feel guilty? Should I be doing more?

I noticed the cop on my tail a block after leaving the house where Star had been murdered. Usually being tailed by the GRPD didn't bother me. If they wanted to waste their time doing it, I really didn't care. But now it irritated me. I didn't mention the tail to Stu.

I drove to River City Lounge in the River City Hotel, one of my regular stops. As we stepped through the door, the blast of Credence Clearwater Revival's latest hit, "Proud

Mary" filled the space. Couples on the dance floor moved to the music.

I turned to catch what Stu was saying over the din when, suddenly, I was pulled to the dance floor and brought face to face with Samantha, a cocktail waitress I'd known for a year. I was too stunned to resist.

I'd always said I couldn't dance. To the good Dutch folks I'd grown up with, dancing was a forbidden worldly pleasure. As adolescents, we joked that pre-marital sex was evil because it could lead to dancing. But often, as I trolled the bars, I'd find myself wishing I were one of the dancers.

Now here I was, dancing with the luscious Samantha, her black uniform showing off her great legs and deep cleavage. I took in her olive skin, dark hair and long lashes."

"Hey, sweetheart, thought you couldn't dance," said Samantha, gyrating her hips and yelling to be heard over the noise.

I tried to move the way I'd watched others do. "You're going to ruin my reputation, Sam," I hollered back.

"Are you kidding?" she said, eyes flashing. "It's way too late for that. Seriously, though, maybe this isn't a good idea. You could ruin my reputation." Then she brought her lips close to my ear. "I read in the paper about you finding the dead girl. Thought you could use some cheering up."

"You certainly took my mind off that for a few minutes. Thanks, I guess."

"Hey, seriously." She took me by the arm. "I have to get back to work but I got a favor to ask." We stepped off the dance floor. "You know I told you about my sister. She got busted for soliciting on South Division. She's at the county jail. I told her about you, and she'd like a visit."

"Okay, Sam. I'll go see her."

"Thanks, honey." She gave me a peck on the cheek. "One of these days I'm going to give you a real kiss. You better be ready." Her eyes flashed again.

I moved to the bar and joined Stu, who looked at me with eyebrows raised. "I suppose that was dance ministry you were doing?"

I laughed. "Yeah. I mean, no. Sam ambushed me."

"I noticed you didn't refuse."

"I'm screwed either way, Stu. What'll people think of a minister dancing with a sexy cocktail waitress? On the other hand, any guy in this place would jump at the chance. So, if I refused, I might as well wear a sign that says 'Super-square street minister.'"

I introduced Stu to the bartender, and, over a beer, answered his questions about the murder. After talking with a couple of high school classmates I frequently ran into here, Stu and I made our retreat while couples danced to José Feliciano's "Light My Fire." I felt tickled that Sam had dragged me out on the dance floor, but I tried not to think about the fire she lit in me.

In my car, I quickly descended back into the lethargy I'd felt earlier. I was sure Stu would understand if I called it a night. Except I'd promised Deacon I'd try to meet him at Koinonia Coffee House, a gathering spot for heads and straights—conventional kids—not far from the Ministry. Besides, Wild Bill was playing his twelve-string and singing at the coffee house. Maybe listening to him would cheer me up a little. In addition, some of the heads knew Star well and might need some support. Maybe someone would have an idea who killed her.

When Stu and I arrived at Koinonia, we found Wild Bill sitting in the far corner of the room on a high stool, strumming and singing Bob Dylan's "Blowin' In the Wind." Decked out in a white shirt embroidered with flowers and with beads draped around his neck, his dark hair hung well below his shoulders. His long beard and his mustache completed his ensemble. Wild Bill had probably ingested every illegal substance known to man, but he played a mean guitar.

As usual on weekends, the room was crowded with straights and heads. The hippie scene had arrived somewhat late in staid, conservative Grand Rapids, as did most fads and fashions. But the flower children here, like elsewhere around the country, flaunted their untraditional appearance, freedom from current sexual mores, use of drugs, and opposition to the Vietnam War. They were full of hope for a tomorrow of peace and love, despite the assassinations of the Kennedy brothers and Martin Luther King.

The coffee house audience sat around a dozen battered tables, and most gave Bill their full attention. Stu and I found an empty table near the door and ordered coffee. I gave myself over to the music, letting it seep into the achy places in my soul.

When Wild Bill finished his set, he joined his girlfriend at a table near the front. Picking up my coffee and motioning Stu to follow, I made my way forward. As the kids at the next table got up to leave, Bill pulled two chairs over.

"Sounding great as usual, man," I said, sitting down. "I really needed your music tonight."

"Thanks." Bill took a sip of coffee. "I'm afraid if I weren't plucking my strings, I'd be sitting home thinking about Star and getting all bent out of shape."

Wild Bill and his girlfriend greeted Stu, a familiar face to them. By the size of their pupils it was obvious the couple was high. I could never tell from Bill's behavior if he was using, but his girl always wore a spaced-out grin and laughed when anyone spoke. She might have been pretty, with her grey eyes and brown hair; but whatever defined her got lost in the haze of her high.

"So, Rob, you going to join us for the anti-war demonstration next week?" asked Bill.

"Wouldn't miss it," I said.

Bill's girlfriend laughed.

Bill gave me a thumbs-up. "How about you, Stu? You covering it?"

"I am."

Bill's girl laughed.

After a few minutes, three other heads came in, pushed an empty table closer to ours, and sat down. One was Deacon. His long blond hair had been parted carefully in the middle.

"Moved into a new crash pad, Rob," said Deacon. He told me where it was. "How about coming next Thursday night for a rap session."

I promised I would.

Bill's girlfriend laughed.

When the subject turned to Star's murder, I asked if anyone had an idea who her killer might be. Everyone shrugged or said they didn't, except Deacon who showed no reaction. Nobody wanted to talk about it.

A few minutes later Deacon walked out with Stu and me. We stood under the light in the parking lot. "What's on your mind, Deacon?" I asked.

"I was hoping we could go someplace where it's easier to talk than here, but if you have to leave, we can get together some other time."

"We could go to my office or to the Windmill Cafe. Stu's tagging along with me tonight, but if you want more privacy—"

"Stu's no problem, as long as I don't have my mother reading about my life in the paper." Deacon grinned.

"Tell you what. After you and Rob finish talking, I'll check out with you what's okay to include in a story and I don't have to use your real name."

"That's cool, man."

The Windmill Café, on Michigan Hill had seen its better days and was no longer owned by a Dutch American. The restaurant displayed black and white photos on it walls of windmills and people dressed in traditional Dutch attire.

After we'd been served, Deacon talked about the direction of his life, the impact of his father's death, and his guilt because his mom didn't approve of his dropping out of college.

"Sounds like you're taking charge of your life," I said.

"Yeah. Except…" Deacon stared out the window. "I know it's probably dumb, but I wish I could help people at the Ministry like you and Nathan do."

"It's not dumb at all," I said, feeling better than I'd felt all evening. "Maybe there is something you can do at the Ministry. I'll get back to you on that." I knew some of the kids confided in Deacon, even some of the gang girls. Maybe Nathan could use Deacon on the volunteer staff.

We talked for a while about the murder, and then Deacon and Stu talked about what Stu would write.

After a pause, Deacon said, "There's something bugging me about Star, Rob."

"What do you mean?"

"I talked to her a few days ago. She seemed nervous. When I asked her what was bothering her, she wouldn't say. She'd usually open up to me when something upset her. I should have pushed her harder."

"I can tell you this, bro," I said. "It's natural to feel guilty, like you should have done more. Believe me, I've been feeling the same way."

"Yeah? Glad I'm not the only one." He was quiet a moment. "It just feels like there's a piece about Star I can't quite get a handle on."

"She talk with you about anything else?"

Deacon looked thoughtful. "She asked me what I thought of Dirk at the gas station next to the Ministry."

"What did you say?"

"I said that we all knew what a jerk he was, and we both laughed."

Nothing new, I thought. I'd heard the kids complain about Dirk's crudeness and hostility more than once.

"Any idea why Star joined the gang?" I asked.

"I think somebody was messing with her. Her dad or a teacher or neighbor or somebody. She never came right out and said it in so many words."

"Messing with her. You mean sexually?"

"Yeah. But maybe I just have an active imagination."

"If I see Detective Johnson, I'll pass your suspicion on."

I didn't want to think about Star being messed with, so I focused on the good feeling I had about Deacon's desire to help at the Ministry. The meeting with him helped me feel I was doing my job again.

Next stop for Stu and me was the parking lot on Fulton Street. As usual during the summer, especially on weekends, the lot was crowded with cars parked at odd angles, small knots of guys and girls sitting in or on the cars or standing near them.

Stu and I walked to where several of the Lost Souls were gathered around Red Feather's rusted out Ford. When I squeezed Red Feather's shoulder, he looked at me and shook his head. The others looked away, probably at a loss as to how to support him in his grief. Gesturing toward Stu, I said to the kids, "Remember the ace Times reporter?"

As the heavies greeted Stu, Outlaw sauntered over from a small group of suburban kids he'd been talking with. Everything about the gang president said "Don't mess with me," from his husky build to his slicked-back, dark hair and his ever–present five o'clock shadow. His denim vest had several short chains sewn to the material and, of course, the gang name on the back.

"Hey, good articles in the paper, man," Outlaw said to Stu.

"Aw, you just liked it because he wrote about you." Cat, Outlaw's girl, nudged him with her elbow and tossed her red ponytail.

Outlaw laughed and put his arm around Cat. "That shows he knows who to talk to."

Deacon and a few other heads we'd seen at the coffee house walked up and greeted the gang members.

"Hey, Father." I heard the call from a kid with another group standing by a late-model, red Chevy.

The teenager who hailed me was a straight, drawn by the magnet of the "circuit." The circuit ran several blocks through downtown, across the Grand River and back to the parking lot where we were gathered. On weekends, hundreds of teens cruised the circuit in their cars, to see and to be seen.

Stu and I walked over to the kids by the Chevy. The one who hailed me said they were students from East High and knew about the Street Ministry.

I heard raised voices and glanced back toward the gang and the heads. Some straight kids had joined them. Suddenly I heard, "I'll show you who's the punk, you motherfucker! You can't treat a guy like shit because he's got long hair." Outlaw ripped off one of the chains from his vest and wrapped it around his left hand. In his right he held a switch-blade, which he brandished toward a tall and well built kid wearing a high school varsity jacket.

The jock also held a knife in his hand, but he looked like he might be sorry for shooting off his mouth. Three of his buddies stood behind him, so he was not about to back down.

I ran over and moved between the two.

CHAPTER 4

The high school kid looked at me in surprise. "Sorry, Father," he said, "but that punk started it."

As I blocked Outlaw with my arm, I heard Deacon say, "Cool it, man. Don't go getting busted for me."

I kept eye contact with the jock and said, "I think it's gone far enough. How about giving me the knife?"

"Not unless he gives you his." High School Guy's eyes tried for defiance, almost made it.

I turned to Outlaw. "Outlaw, would you please give me your weapons?"

He was silent for a moment, probably relishing the drama. Then he said, "Okay, since Father Rob is askin' me."

I managed to keep a straight face at Outlaw's calling me Father Rob.

Holding on to Outlaw's knife and chain in my left hand, I extended my right for the other weapon.

The young man gave me his knife and turned to his friends. "Let's split," he said, and they moseyed to a turquoise Plymouth convertible with its top down. The jock squealed out of the parking lot, getting the last word.

"Thanks, Outlaw," I said. "Took guts to be the first to give up your weapons."

"Shit, I don't need to get busted again for assault. Specially with the cops thinkin' I killed Star."

"I have a question for you," I said.

"You wanna know where I was when Star was murdered. Red Feather and me got into a hassle. I split to the gravel pit by myself and got plastered, so I ain't got nobody to back me up."

I'd heard about the gravel pit out on the river road where the gang liked to swim and party.

"Has Detective Johnson or Kincaid questioned you?"

"Oh yeah. I thought that son-of-a-bitch, Johnson, was gonna lock me up."

So, Outlaw didn't have an alibi. Still, I didn't believe he was the murderer. Of course, I could be wrong. "Any idea who killed Star?"

He shook his head. "Wasn't Mad Dog. He liked Star. Plus he respects Red Feather."

"What were you and Red Feather fighting about?"

Outlaw leaned close and covertly pointed a thumb toward the newest gang member, standing several feet away. "He's a good kid, but he's afraid of his own shadow. He's on probation with the gang, and I wanted to boot him, but Red Feather says the kid needs the gang. That's what Red Feather and me was fightin' about."

As the Souls moved off, Stu and I returned to my car.

"How'd you stay so cool in that confrontation back there?" asked Stu.

"Usually in a situation like that, both kids are scared of getting hurt or hurting someone and looking for a way to get out of the mess without losing face. Outlaw knew I was nearby and spoke loudly enough for me to hear. Probably figured he could gain some tough guy points without things getting out of hand. Did you notice he called me Father? He never calls me that."

"So what are you going to do with the weapons?"

"I don't know. Maybe I'll use them for show-and-tell on my speaking gigs in the churches." As I reached down and stashed them under the front seat of my car, I noticed how much Outlaw's switchblade looked like one I'd carried in Cicero. I wondered what had happened to mine.

After visiting another bar, Stu and I pulled up at Memorial Park behind two police cars with their flashers on. The park was a couple of blocks from the Ministry and another place the kids hung out. I hurried into the park and Stu hustled after me. Four cops had three of the Souls standing spread-eagled against the war memorial. Other kids stood nearby, watching. As Stu and I approached, Outlaw turned his head toward us. One of the cops pushed Outlaw's face hard against the memorial and said, "Don't move, punk, or I'll bust you."

I stepped forward. "What's the problem, officer?" I addressed the cop who had his hand on Outlaw's back. Before the officer could answer, I said, "I'm Reverend Rob Vander Laan from the Street Ministry, and this is Stu Peterson from the Times. Anything we can do to help?"

Okay, so it wasn't a genuine offer of assistance.

The cop glanced at my collar and then took a long hard look at Stu. Finally he said, "We were just warning these, ah, hoodlums that they'd better not bother anyone. Been a bunch of complaints about the gang. And there's been a murder. These delinquents are frightening the good citizens of this community."

The cop removed his hand from Outlaw's back and told the Souls they'd better clean up their act. Then the cops left the park.

"Fuckin' pigs." said Outlaw, wiping blood from his nose with the back of his hand.

I was thinking much the same. The three heavies moved off, the other kids following.

"How would you feel about me writing this up?" asked Stu.

"Up to you, but I'm thinking not," I said. "Might gain the Ministry a couple of points with the GRPD if you don't."

* * *

I jerked a pillowcase off a pillow and slipped it over my head. I made claws with my hands and growled in Andy's direction.

Andy squealed and bounded off my bed as I reached for him.

"No, Daddy. I want to be a monster, too."

I put the other pillowcase over Andy's head.

"Rrrrrrrrr!" said the little monster.

"Hey, you monsters," said Jackie from the doorway. "The big monster has to shower. You, little monster, have to take care of your toys before Grandma and Grandpa get here for dinner."

I stumbled to the door, claws raised and growled mightily at Jackie. Andy, at my side, did the same.

Jackie laughed and pushed me away.

"Oh, babe, I forgot to tell you last night," I said, pulling off the pillowcase and tossing it on the bed. "I'm going to see Star's parents at two."

"You'd better get a move on. We'll eat as soon as my folks get here."

After I showered and dressed, I found Andy downstairs, busy with one of his rituals. With great care he lined up his trucks, largest to smallest, in a perfectly neat row.

By the time I finished tossing the salad, Jackie's parents arrived. They came into the kitchen, Jackie's dad looking at a section of the Times he'd picked up from the couch in the living room.

"I'll bet you guys didn't get to church again," said Jackie's mom. Without waiting for a reply, she added, "Maybe it's time to move on and become a real minister, Rob."

Used to hearing this suggestion from my mother-in-law and a few others, I seldom chose to defend myself, but Jackie bristled. "Rob is a real minister. You came to his ordination last year. Have you forgotten?"

"You know what I mean, honey. He should have a regular church. Did you decide about the call to Washington Avenue, Rob?"

"No. Can't rush the Spirit on these things, Mom."

Jackie rolled her eyes at me.

"How are you coping with that murder business, Rob?" Jackie's dad asked, changing the subject.

The image of Star's bloody body swam before my eyes. "I guess I'm doing okay, Dad. It's hard for me to stay focused on my work, but I'm told that, if I keep talking about it, it's supposed to get easier."

"If you need an ear, don't hesitate to ask." He held up the Sunday paper. "The story about 'God's Bartender' is, uh, interesting."

This was news to me since I hadn't seen the paper, but I was mostly surprised that Stu had gotten it in before deadline.

Jackie grinned. "I'll have a Reformed martini, big guy."

"God's bartender?" Sharon took the paper from Bert. "Oh, for Pete's sake."

Andy tugged at my pants. "What's a Reformed martini, Daddy?"

A few minutes later we gathered around the dining room table where I asked my father-in-law to say grace. The Dutch tradition of a big Sunday noon dinner was one of my favorites, and the pot roast tasted great.

The phone rang halfway through the meal. I excused myself and reached for the phone on the wall. "Hello. This is Rob Vander Laan."

"When you answer the phone, you should identify yourself as Reverend Vander Laan. I've told you that before."

"Hello, Mother." I grimaced, as I realized I should have called my parents.

"You should have called us," my mother continued. "We had to hear about you finding the body of that girl from someone in our church who's brother is a Grand Rapids police officer."

The Dutch grapevine. I hated it, especially in my adolescence when my father was informed about my every sin before I even returned home from sinning. I vowed never to live in a Dutch enclave after I was on my own. Yet here I was, living in Grand Rapids, the Jerusalem of the Christian Reformed Church.

Before I could reply, Mother continued. "And then, this morning, someone else from Grand Rapids called and read us the article on 'God's Bartender.' I've never been so humiliated. Maybe that dead girl is a sign that you should take the call to Washington Avenue."

I almost told her I was declining the call but bit my tongue. "I know you think I should take the Washington Avenue call, but I need more time with it. Is Dad on the extension?"

"Hi, son." I always had to ask before he'd speak. "How are you holding up? Did you know the girl pretty well?"

"I guess I'm doing okay, Dad." But I wasn't, really. "Yes, I knew her pretty well. I'm visiting her parents this afternoon, so I should get back to my dinner."

As I returned to the table, Jackie's mom said, "See, Rob, your mother and I—"

"Not another word, Mom!" interrupted Jackie.

* * *

I dreaded my visit to Star's parents. Nevertheless, dressed in a tan leisure suit and a dark brown turtleneck, I made the drive after dinner. The sound of Pete Seeger's "Turn! Turn! Turn!" on a local radio station soothed my soul.

I easily found the brick ranch in the modest suburb of Kentwood. Corey greeted me at the door, dark circles under his eyes and stooped posture, a silent testimony to his grief. Alice was seated on the couch with a box of tissues at her side, eyes red. Corey indicated a chair for me across from the couch as he sat down beside Alice and took her hand. On the table next to the couch was a photograph of a young man in military uniform.

"Your son?" I asked, studying the portrait.

"He was killed in Viet Nam a year and a half ago," said Cory.

Two children killed. I couldn't begin to imagine. Seeing Alice and Corey's grief-stricken faces brought the sadness and horror of finding Star's body back to the surface for me. But my experience paled beside theirs. I took a couple of calming breaths, looking at the coffee table. "I'm not sure what to say." After a moment I looked up. "I told you on the phone how sorry I am for your loss. Thanks for seeing me."

Alice's words hit me like a quiet explosion. "Why did this have to happen, Rob? Bad enough dealing with her death, but she was murdered! We asked you to look out for her."

My gaze returned to the coffee table. I had no answer for Alice.

After a moment Corey cleared his throat. "Let's hear what he has to say, Alice. Go ahead, Rob."

I choked down the guilt and sadness I felt and looked up. "I want to tell you a little about Star, the Susan I knew. She seemed seriously troubled when she first started hanging out downtown. For the last several months, though, she's been a positive leader. It probably won't surprise you that she treated the other downtown kids with respect. Some of them talked with her about their problems, and she sometimes talked with me about what advice to give them."

Tears spilled down Alice's cheeks and Corey's eyes glistened.

I took a breath. "The next thing I have to say might be hard to hear. She had a boyfriend downtown. He's part Cherokee and the vice president of the Lost Souls, the gang Susan belonged to."

Alice smiled a sad smile, no more anger in her eyes. "Susan brought Red Feather here and introduced him to us. She said it was your idea to come over with him."

"It was a shock," said Corey, "to see the two of them popping in the back door holding hands, wearing those gang vest things. Colors, she called them. But after we talked for an hour, we couldn't help but like Red Feather, even though he's a gang member."

"I'm glad Susan brought Red Feather to meet you," I said." He and Susan were a good influence on the other kids and made my job easier."

"Rob," said Corey, "do you think one of the Lost Souls murdered our daughter? Two detectives were here. I got the distinct impression they think one of the gang members did it."

"I really don't know, Corey, but I doubt it." His question made me realize Star's killer wasn't necessarily someone from the downtown scene.

"Do you have any idea who might have killed her if it wasn't one of the gang?" asked Corey.

"I don't."

I studied Corey, remembering what Deacon had said about somebody messing with Star. The idea of the man sitting across from me molesting his daughter seemed preposterous, but what did I know? I thought about raising the issue but decided to leave that to Sid Johnson.

Alice said, "Susan and Red Feather had supper with us while they were here, and they both ate like they hadn't eaten for a week. Said things were a little tight right now. To think that Susan wasn't getting enough to eat …"

"Sometimes it's hand-to-mouth for the gang," I said. "Depends on whether anybody has a job or any of them have done day labor."

"It was good of you to come and tell us about Susan," said Alice. "I'm sorry about what I said earlier."

"No apology necessary."

Just then a little girl with a sad, sweet face, who looked about eight years old, came quietly into the room. "Hi, Judy," said Corey. "Come and meet Reverend Vander Laan, Remember Susan talking about him?"

"Susie liked you," Judy said. "She told me all about you."

"I liked her too, Judy. I liked her a lot."

"Come sit by me, sweetie," said Alice. She put an arm around her daughter.

After a moment I said, "I have something of Susan's, and I'm wondering if I can give it to Judy." I reached into my pocket, took out the chain with the peace sign on it and held it up. "Susan dropped this in my office last week. The clasp is broken."

Judy's eyes lit up as she jumped off the couch and took the necklace from me. She held it up to her neck. "Thanks, Reverend Vander Laan."

"Most everybody calls me Rob. If it's okay with your folks, you can call me that, too."

"Thanks Rob," she said with a sideways look at Corey. "I'll take good care of the necklace."

Corey cleared his throat and looked at Alice, who nodded. "There's something we'd like to ask you, Rob. We talked it over, and we talked to our minister, too. We'd like you to say a few words about Susan at the funeral on Tuesday."

"I'd be honored. I'd like to ask you something, too. How would you feel about some of the downtown people coming to the funeral?"

"They'll be welcome as far as we're concerned," said Alice.

I wondered if the murderer would show up at the funeral like in the movies.

CHAPTER 5

I woke late Monday morning in a cold sweat. I lay there, listening to the voices of Jackie and Andy drift up from downstairs. I couldn't remember my dream, but I knew it had been about Star's murder. I made a beeline for the shower, as if I could wash away the reality of her death. I debated mentioning the nightmare to Jackie, but decided not to.

Jackie was off on Mondays, and I normally took the day off, too, so we were usually both home. She worked as a nurse three days a week at a medical office. Jackie's mom or my mother took care of Andy on the days we both worked. That made it possible for me to sleep in most mornings after working late.

As I sat at my desk in the study later, thinking about what I'd say at Star's funeral the next day, the phone rang. Lydia, my seventy-year-old secretary, said that Outlaw and Red Feather were at the Ministry. They wanted a meeting at Drop-in that evening to talk about the murder investigation and the funeral.

After supper I drove to the Ministry. Drop-in was packed with heavies, heads, and several straights, all Drop-in regulars. Most of the kids sat on the floor while some lounged on chairs around the table. Nathan, Lydia and three volunteers were scattered among the kids. I saluted Mad Dog whom I hadn't seen since the night of the murder.

"Okay, Outlaw and Red Feather," I said, "you guys asked for the meeting. Anything you want to say to start things off?"

Pain showed in Red Feather's eyes. His body jerked a little as if he was shaking something off. "I think the first thing to talk about is the funeral. I heard it's goin' to be tomorrow at Star's church, and a bunch of us wanna go. We wondered what you think about that, Rob."

I directed my response to the whole group. "Mrs. Wynsma, Star's mom, said you will all be welcome. After the funeral there will be a caravan of cars to the cemetery. Then back to the church basement for refreshments. Don't hesitate to talk with Star's parents afterwards," I added. "And be sure to say hi to Judy, Star's little sister."

"If there's nothin' else about the funeral," said Outlaw, "can we talk about Star's murder?"

"Go ahead," I said.

He shifted in his seat. "The pigs seem to think Mad Dog or me did it. Don't they have no other suspects?"

"I don't know. All of us in this room are probably suspects till we're cleared. So the cops are doing their job."

Outlaw wore a dark scowl. "You sound like you're on the pigs' side." He stood up. "Fuck it," he said, leaving the room and heading out of the building. Mad Dog followed him.

After a moment of uncomfortable silence, I said, "I expect Outlaw's not the only one who's mad. I wonder if it might help if we talked about Star, what we remember about her."

It took a few minutes, but after Nathan and one of the volunteers shared their memories, several of the kids opened up. One of the girls talked about the time Star had brought a birthday cake to Drop-in for her right after she'd tried to commit suicide. Another of the girls mentioned the time Star had freaked out when Nathan came out of the bathroom wearing a vampire mask and how hard they'd all laughed. Red Feather told how he'd met Star at the gravel pit the night one of the girls had introduced her to the gang. There was a small meteor shower that night, and Star had gotten her nickname. Another of the girls said Star always knew what to say to her when she was bummed out about something.

After a while I asked if there was anything else. No one spoke and I ended the meeting.

I entered my office and sat down at my desk. I wanted to be alone. Most of the kids filed out to the street, with a few staying to listen to Wild Bill strum and sing. I was watching the exodus through my front window when my secretary came in. I found Lydia's solid build and steady blue eyes reassuring. She wore a flower print dress and, as usual, her gray hair was pinned in a bun.

"Seems odd to see you here at night," I said.

"I like being here in Drop-in when I'm not working the front desk. Maybe I'll talk to Nathan about coming in more often. I wanted to let you know that Red Feather wants to talk with you. He knows Monday is supposed to be your day off, so he said he'd check with you at the funeral."

I stood "Okay. I should get going."

"Not so fast, buster. Sit." She peered at me.

"Will it take long?"

She shrugged.

I checked my watch. "Let me call Jackie and check with her." I called and told her that the meeting was over and Lydia wanted to talk.

"It's supposed to be your day off," said Jackie, irritation in her voice. She worried about my safety in my work sometimes, and the murder had probably increased her concern. I suspected that was behind her irritation. Usually she liked having time alone at home after Andy was in bed.

"If you want me home, I'll talk with Lydia another time."

"No, go ahead."

"Andy doing okay?" I asked.

"His asthma flared up. I gave him his med, and he's better now."

I hung up and turned my attention to Lydia.

"This can wait if you need to get home," she said.

"Nope. Jackie's cool with it.

She smiled. "I miss your little guy. Haven't seen him since I was with you at Jackie's parents' farm." Then her look turned serious. "I've been wondering how you're doing with finding Star's body. Don't just tell me you're fine. You're playing with your beard again. You always do that when something's bugging you."

I folded my hands on my desk. I didn't want to talk about it, but I knew I should. "I honestly don't know. Sometimes things seem almost normal, and then I see her lying there."

"Are you talking about it with anyone?"

"Yes. Jackie and Nathan."

"Any nightmares?"

"I woke up in a cold sweat this morning. Couldn't remember the dream."

"Did you tell Jackie?"

"No, I didn't want to bother her."

Lydia's scowl told me it was the wrong answer. "That's a fine how-do-you-do. Tell her. You keep talking about it, and you'll learn to live with it. My late husband, God rest his soul, finally started telling me about his war experiences. It was hard at first, but he said it helped a lot." Her face softened. "I'd like to be one of the people you can talk to."

"I'd like that." I felt my body relax. We sat in companionable silence. Then I leaned back in my chair. "Now, a question for you. What are you doing at the Street Ministry when you could be taking it easy and enjoying retirement?"

"Gives me a reason to get up every day. I never had any kids." Lydia went quiet for a moment. "Let's just say I did some things I shouldn't have when I was young and foolish. After that I couldn't have kids. I always felt like I had an empty place in me because of that. I wish the kids would stop calling me Gram, though. Makes me feel old."

A few minutes later I walked down the steps of the Ministry, glad I'd stayed to talk with Lydia. I almost bumped into Detectives Johnson and Kincaid on the sidewalk.

"Sorry," I said.

"Go ahead, Kincaid," grumped Johnson. "It's your idea."

"We'd like to ascertain some background about you," Kincaid said. "We'll only detain you briefly. We know you grew up in Sioux Center, Iowa, Cicero, Illinois, and Holland, Michigan—places where your father served churches. We know you were a teacher at Christian High for some years before you entered seminary. We know you did a year of internship in a ghetto church in the Chicago area between your last two years of seminary."

Why the heck had they been checking up on me? Was I a suspect? Well, I'd told the kids we all were.

Kincaid looked at me closely. "What I am perplexed about is why a clergyman from a conservative Dutch Reformed denomination is working in a liberal ministry like this." He gestured toward my building.

"In my last year of seminary," I said, "I became acquainted with the Street Ministry and got hooked on it." Perhaps "got hooked" was a poor choice of words, given the heads and their drug use.

"Indeed. What *hooked* you?" asked Kincaid.

What could I say without sounding preachy? "The thing that caught me was the focus here on loving and accepting people as they are. Society looks down on most of the people we work with. If Jesus were living in Grand Rapids today, I figure this is where he'd be. Besides, I was socially and politically asleep through most of the sixties. Some of the protesting in our country reminds me of the Old Testament prophets. I don't want to miss this time holed up in a Dutch ghetto."

So much for not sounding preachy, I thought.

"I don't need a sermon," said Johnson. "What I want to know is why Susan Wynsma joined the gang."

"Star told me it wasn't safe for her at home, but she wouldn't say any more about it."

"Any guess as to why it wasn't safe for her?"

I reported Deacon's suspicion that Star had been molested.

* * *

In the far corner of the church parking lot the next day there were three old cars with about twenty of the downtown kids gathered by them. I parked next to them. I had debated about wearing my clerical shirt to the funeral. It was not the way Christian Reformed ministers dressed, aside from a couple of our clergy who served racially mixed churches in other cities. The street kids who came to the funeral, however, might be more at ease if they saw me wearing my collar. And it was the way Star knew me.

I surveyed my street congregation. Most were surprisingly well dressed. No colors, no shirts or jackets with peace signs; some blue jeans, a few sport coats and ties and dresses that suggested a recent trip to the Goodwill Store.

When Nathan arrived with Lydia, we all paraded across the lot and into the church. I was aware of the looks we got and the whispered conversations. I knew the street kids noticed too. Red Feather, walking next to me whispered, "Let's talk after the funeral."

Was it about Star's murder? I wanted to know right away, but I told myself to be patient.

We all sat together half way down on the left side of the aisle. The sanctuary continued to fill. The organist quietly played old hymns. The aroma of flowers surrounding the casket permeated the air. Star's family and close relatives, entering from the front, took their seats in the pews closest to the pulpit. Seeing Judy, Star's little sister, holding her mom's hand and looking so serious just about did me in.

I'd been eight years old when I'd gone to my first funeral. Grandpa had lived with us for five years, and I used to sit on the floor by his chair to listen to his stories about life in the old country. The memory I treasured most was that no matter how much trouble I might be in with my parents, I was always okay with Grandpa. At his funeral no one paid attention to me, except for a lady who told me I should be happy because Grandpa was in a better place. When she turned her back, I stuck out my tongue at her.

I looked away from Judy. John Vanden Berg, the pastor, took his place behind the pulpit. Both our fathers served churches in Holland. He and I had been high school classmates, and we'd been very competitive with each other. John outshone me in basketball and on the debate team, but I'd beaten him in the election for student body president in our senior year. I didn't think he ever forgave me for that. I kept my eyes on him during the service, but his words barely registered. I kept seeing Star's body lying on the floor of the gang's apartment.

In closing, John looked directly at us, the downtown crew, as he warned of eternal damnation. He was blessedly brief.

When I took his place behind the pulpit, I looked first at Star's family. Judy smiled at me and I almost lost it again. I shifted my gaze to the Street Ministry contingent and then scanned the rest of the gathering as I drew a breath.

"Her name was Susan Wynsma," I began. "I only learned that recently. Downtown we called her Star, and that's just what she was to us." I made some comments to the downtown crew, to the teens from Susan's church, and to Cory and Alice.

Then I smiled at Star's sister. "Judy, I see you're wearing the necklace with the peace sign that Susan wore. That's another thing we can remember her for," I said, taking in the rest of the congregation. "She brought a little bit of peace into the lives of many of us.

"She was a gift from God, reminding us, without ever putting it into words, that we are acceptable and deserving of respect.

"Now she's gone. Snatched from us. Murdered. We may be devastated with grief, outraged. We may feel a great emptiness. We may wonder how a loving God could allow this. We may need to walk in those places for a while. But we walk with the memory of Star, a girl we were blessed to know. Perhaps we will try to be more like her."

After a brief graveside service, we returned to the church for a light luncheon. I expressed my condolences to Corey and Alice and then talked for a few minutes with Judy. Seeing me with the Wynsmas, the downtown young people came over and joined us. Some talked for a moment to Judy, who became quite animated. Apparently, she enjoyed being the center of their attention.

Then, as the downtown kids moved away, Alice introduced me to a few friends and relatives. I was ready to leave when she delayed me with an introduction to Warren Van Boven and his wife. Warren, about forty, had flaming red hair and a severely pockmarked face. His wife barely made eye contact with me. "They've lived next door forever, and they're members of our church," said Alice. "Warren was a real friend to Susan."

The man extended a damp hand to me. "Nice to meet you. We have to run. Sorry. I have to get back to work." Warren took his wife's elbow and hustled her away.

When I got out to the parking lot, anxious to talk with Red Feather, I noted with frustration that the downtown people had left. To my surprise, however, I found Red Feather waiting for me in the passenger seat of my car. Outlaw sat in the backseat.

"Been wantin' to tell you this for a couple days," said Red Feather as I got in.

"I'm sorry we haven't been able to connect before."

When Red Feather looked at me, his eyes shot sparks of pure hatred. "I wanted to tell you that some perverted neighbor guy of Star's used to force her to fuck him."

I sat in stunned silence. I couldn't think of anything to say. Finally, I said, "Tell me more."

"It went on for a couple of years. She made me promise not to tell nobody."

"Is that why she started hanging out downtown, to get away from him?"

"Yeah."

"Why didn't she tell her folks?"

"She sure as hell wanted to, but the motherfucker swore he'd hurt Judy real bad if Star ratted him out."

"She told you all this?" I was having trouble breathing.

"Yeah. I wanted to beat the crap out of the bastard, but she begged me not to do nothin'."

"Why are you telling me now?"

"Star said this neighbor used to talk about what he did with hookers. She saw him downtown last Friday night, and he tried to get her into his car to go have some fun with some whore. Star told him she'd scream if he touched her. She said she was gonna tell her folks and the cops about him."

"Wasn't she worried about his threat to hurt Judy?"

"Star told me Judy was at her aunt's in Cadillac, so she figured it was a good time to turn the cocksucker in."

"Do you think this guy could have murdered her?"

"Yeah, I do. I'm so pissed, I wanna beat the goddamn truth out of him."

"What's the guy's name?"

Red Feather's shoulders sagged. "She wouldn't tell me."

"You have to tell the cops."

"Yeah, I know, but Johnson's a racist pig. He jumped on me because I'm Indian. Everybody backed up my alibi, so he had to let me go. I'll talk to him, but you gotta be there."

Outlaw hadn't said a word, but I felt his presence.

While we talked, the lot had emptied, except for a few cars. "Let's go to the Ministry," I said, "and call to see if Johnson is in."

From my office, I called the police station. Johnson sounded stressed out and said he only had a minute. I gave him a nutshell version of what Red Feather had reported.

"I don't want anybody to say another word about this," said Johnson. "I'll leave a message at your place as to when Kincaid and I can get there tonight to talk to Red Feather."

I hung up the phone. "The detectives will meet us here tonight," I said to Red Feather. "Johnson asked us not to talk about this with anyone. Where are you going to be later?"

Red Feather glanced at Outlaw. "Just hangin' with the gang—here, the park, the lot."

"I'll find you. Check at the front desk in case I leave you a message."

"Oh, and, Rob, my grandmother in Oklahoma ain't doin' so hot again. I might have to get back there." I knew he'd lived with his grandmother until moving to Grand Rapids to stay with an aunt when he was sixteen. He always spoke of his grandmother with a fondness that touched me. "I hate to take off with what's goin' on," he continued.

The thought of leaving Outlaw to lead the gang by himself probably worried Red Feather as much as his grandmother's health.

"Doubt if Johnson will even let me go see Granny," he said.

"If you need to use the phone in my office to call your grandmother, let me know."

"But it's long distance."

"I know. That's okay."

"Really? Thanks."

As Red Feather heaved himself out of the chair, Outlaw stood up and said, "Sorry I went off on you at the meeting, Rob. Johnson questioned me three times, and, like I told you, I ain't got no alibi."

I was too preoccupied with the news about Star to say anything supportive to Outlaw.

When the two gang leaders left, I sat back, feeling horror and anger deep in my bones. Star would have been fifteen or sixteen when she was being molested. Must have been about the time her brother was killed in Nam. I wanted to break something. I looked at the paperweight on my desk. I felt like pitching it through the window.

Then I thought back to the neighbor Star's parents had introduced me to after the funeral. What was his name? Van or Vander or Vanden something. I snorted. Big help! I remembered the joke in the Dutch community that if you had one address book for A through U and another for V through Z, you must be Dutch.

Van Boven. That was it. Warren Van Boven. I could clearly visualize the pocked face and red hair. Could Van Boven be the neighbor who molested Star? Could he have killed her?

CHAPTER 6

"Does Red Feather know who killed Star?" demanded Lydia.

I'd stopped at the front desk on my way out of the Ministry and told her that Johnson would leave a message as to when he could meet Red Feather and me.

"No. Johnson just needs to talk with us about some things related to the murder."

"You're not going to tell me?" Irritation in her voice. A look that almost made me spill it. "You shouldn't hide things from me, Rob. How can I do my job if you keep me in the dark?"

Sometimes it seemed as though Lydia knew all the secrets of the staff and kids. No wonder we referred to her as Communication Central.

"I'll tell you more when I can. I'm going to the jail now to visit a sister of someone who works at one of my night ministry stops."

Before heading to the jail, I pulled up to the gas pumps at the station next door to the Ministry. Dirk Boyle shuffled over. There was something off about him. Stocky-built, in his thirties, wearing the worn Detroit Tigers baseball cap he always wore, he leaned down to my open window, eyes aimed toward my back seat. "Howdy, Reverend," he said.

I'd given up on asking him to call me Rob. "I need a quart of oil."

Dirk raised the hood, then went into the station to get the oil. I remembered Star had asked Deacon what he thought of Dirk. I wondered now why she'd asked.

When Dirk returned with the oil, I got out and said, "How's Harley doing?"

Harley was Dirk's boss. The two often got upset at the kids cutting through the station on their way to the Ministry or the park. They also got angry when our staff parked briefly in spaces reserved for their customers, even when it was just to run into our building for a minute. We didn't do that anymore, mostly.

Dirk finished topping off the oil. "Harley's okay. Cops have any luck catching the kid that killed that girl?" he asked, studying my shoes.

"What makes you think one of the kids killed her?"

"All these kids are trouble-makers. Wouldn't trust 'em any further'n I could throw 'em."

As I paid him he said, "You better find out why your car's taking oil."

On the way to the jail, I pondered the question of who murdered Star. Multiple stab wounds sounded psychotic. Arnold? The loner. I remembered the haunted look I sometimes saw in his eyes. I should mention him to Johnson.

Or rage and fear might have motivated the killing. Maybe Warren Van Boven killed Star to keep her from exposing him. *If* he was the neighbor who had molested her.

I tried to imagine Outlaw as the murderer. I wondered how he felt about Red Feather's powerful influence on several of the gang members. Could he be so jealous that he killed Star? I didn't buy it.

As for Mad Dog, I still had a gut feeling his story at the apartment was true. Of course, my gut could be wrong about both him and Outlaw.

In ten minutes I was at the county jail. My face was familiar there, and I was quickly admitted into the visitors' room where I took a seat at one of the tables. A few moments later Sam's sister entered, wearing a green prisoner's dress. She had dark hair like her sister and brown eyes—a street-worn version of Samantha.

I stood up and held out my hand. "I'm Rob Vander Laan. Samantha asked me to come."

Her grip was dry and firm. "Thanks for coming, Reverend. Sam was here Monday and said you'd come."

"Call me Rob," I said as we sat down. "How long before you get out?"

"Three weeks," she said. "I got thirty days and a hundred-dollar fine." She pulled back a little in her chair. "You aren't going to try to convert me, are you?"

"Did Sam tell you that? I wouldn't put it past her. I'm here to get acquainted with you and to listen."

"Yeah, Sam did say that, but I thought she might be kidding. She said you almost had her converted, but she laughed when she said it."

I remembered my encounter with Sam on the dance floor at the bar. Who was converting whom?

"So, how is it going in here?"

"Oh, it's great fun. A vacation from working the street." Then she sobered. "Sam did tell you I got busted for soliciting, didn't she? But, seriously," she said pushing her hair away from her eyes, "the worst thing is the boredom. Time just drags, if you know what I mean."

What did I know about being locked up in jail?

She talked about her childhood in Newaygo, north of Grand Rapids. "Sam and I weren't close," she said. "I'm a couple of years older and bullied her. And Dad—let's not talk about him. I'll just say by the time I was twelve, I figured I had to protect Sam from that asshole."

I stifled a shiver of rage, wondering whether she had been molested as a child. Clearly, she'd been abused in some way. And what about Sam? Had her sister really succeeded in protecting her? "Sounds like it was miserable at home."

"You got that right. I split when I was seventeen and been on my own since. It's better than being around the asshole."

We sat in silence for a moment.

She crossed her legs and arms. "Sam told me about you finding that dead girl. Must have been a real downer."

"It was."

"Cops catch the murderer yet?"

"No."

She gave a cynical laugh. "No way are they gonna work their butts off to find a street kid's killer."

She had just put words to my fear.

The announcement for the end of visiting hours came over the public address system, and we stood.

"I'll come back to see you if you want me to," I said.

She said she'd like that. "Careful on the street," she added. "It's a jungle out there."

* * *

"Hey, Nathan," I said. "What's happening?" After a visit to a coffee house in one of the suburbs, I'd stopped at the Ministry and found Nathan sitting at the front desk.

Nathan bowed from his chair. "Greetings, Exalted One."

I raised an eyebrow, but I was used to his teasing.

He pushed back in his chair. "Found Gimp crashing upstairs last night after we closed. I've suspected it for a while. He always seems to disappear shortly before we turn the kids out."

"Did you make him leave?"

"No. We talked for a while. He doesn't have a place right now. I told him he could stay the night, but that it probably wasn't the greatest idea for him to be sleeping here."

"Sounds like you were less than crystal clear with him about it."

"You're very perceptive. They teach you that at seminary?"

"I'm not really concerned about it either, as long as he's not doing dope or drinking or stealing anything. But I wouldn't want the place to turn into a crash pad."

I walked into Drop-In where a dozen kids sat with two volunteers. From a portable radio belonging to one of the kids came the sound of *Aquarius* by the Fifth Dimension. "Seen anything of Red Feather?" I asked.

"I think he's in the lot," said Wild Bill's girlfriend. A straight answer, no giggles. She wasn't high yet.

Checking my watch, I saw it was almost time for the detectives to arrive. I hustled to the parking lot where I found Red Feather talking with two black members of the gang. Red Feather and I walked back to my office, the gang leader rambling about Star, slurring his words and smelling of beer. This was not going to help his credibility with Johnson. When we entered my office, the detectives were already seated in front of my desk.

Johnson stood. "Got here a little early. The guy at the front desk said to wait in here."

"Evening, Detectives," I said. "I think you both know Red Feather."

I brought in another chair. Red Feather sat down. He moved his chair a couple of inches back. Detective Johnson, sitting next to him, did the same. The detectives and Red Feather eyed each other warily as I rounded my desk and sat down behind it.

"Red Feather told me some interesting things today, Detectives," I said. "It's possible they relate to Star's death. He's agreed to tell you."

"I'm all ears," said Johnson with more than a hint of sarcasm.

Red Feather bristled at Johnson's tone..

"Go ahead, Red Feather," I said.

He looked at me and I nodded. After a moment he repeated for the cops what Star had told him about her neighbor. Red Feather spoke carefully, trying, unsuccessfully, to sound sober. Listening to the story again about Star's neighbor, I felt the same rage I'd felt previously. The emotion triggered a memory from third grade. In my mind I could see the bully on the playground terrorizing a younger, smaller kid. The bully was in fourth grade. Teachers had to pull me off the bully, and I had to stay after school for a week.

Kincaid took notes. He glanced up at Red Feather. "Do you know the name of the neighbor?"

"Star didn't tell me."

"Why didn't you tell us right away?" asked Johnson.

"Star made me promise not to tell nobody. After I started to get over being so freaked out about her murder, I remembered it. Figured I'd better tell Rob. This afternoon was the first chance I got."

Kincaid and Johnson both looked at me and I nodded.

"Okay, Red Feather," said Johnson. "Appreciate the information."

When Red Feather left the room, I said, "I might know the name of this neighbor." I told the detectives about meeting Warren Van Boven at Star's funeral. "Of course I really don't know if that's the neighbor Star was referring to."

"Even *if* what Red Feather says is true," said Johnson skeptically, "it's only hearsay. Maybe we'll check on this Van Boven and re-canvass the neighbors, if we have time. Anyways, I think one of us already interviewed him."

Kincaid paged through his notebook. "Correct. I spoke with the gentleman."

I thought of Sam's sister's words at the jail: "No way are they gonna work their butts off to find a street kid's killer."

* * *

The phone in the study jolted me awake. I checked the clock on the bedside table: 2:30 a.m. Unusual, but it happened occasionally. I hurried to the phone in the study.

"We need to talk," Arnold said. "Now. It's about Star."

Jackie rolled over when I came back into the bedroom. "Who was that?" she asked, surprisingly alert.

"Just one of the kids in a crisis. I'll see you later." I dressed quickly and drove to the address Arnold had given me in a working class neighborhood on the northeast side, not far from downtown. Arnold, a short wiry man in his mid-twenties, dressed in jeans and a jacket that was too heavy for the warm night, waited under the street lamp. He slid into the car. No apology about the lateness or calling me at home.

"Just drive," he said.

"Any place special?"

"Yeah, get on the expressway toward Lansing."

I didn't like the sound of that. "Why don't we go someplace for coffee?"

Arnold's voice turned threatening. "See this?" I looked down and saw a large hunting knife in his hand. "The freeway," he said.

As I turned on to the highway, I had a quick flash of my body being dumped in a field. Then I glanced at the gas gauge and saw it was on empty. I was glad I hadn't noticed it when I stopped at the station for oil the previous afternoon. "We've got two problems that we need to discuss, Arnold,"

I said calmly. "The first is that we're almost out of gas. Not much open this time of night, so we'll have to go back to the gas station where we got on the expressway. Okay?"

Arnold leaned over to check the gauge. "I guess."

"The second problem," I said in the same matter-of-fact tone, "is that I don't like you holding a knife in your hand. It makes it hard for me to concentrate on my driving. How about giving it to me?"

Silence for what seemed a long time. Then, without a word, Arnold handed the knife to me.

Stashing it under my seat, I exited the highway and headed back.

At the gas station the attendant approached the car. "Fill it with regular?"

"Please."

He started the hose, then returned to my open window. "Can I check your oil?"

"No, it's okay."

"A lot of people don't check it, but you have to do that regularly or you can have some serious engine problems."

"I know what you mean."

Was I really having this mundane interaction with the attendant moments after my passenger had threatened me with a weapon?

As I paid for the gas, the attendant asked, "Stamps?"

"Thanks." Bizarre, I thought, taking the stamps to add to the collection in the glove compartment for later redemption at the store. But if I didn't get them, I'd have to answer to She-Who-Always-Gets-the-Best-Deals.

"So, Arnold," I said, "how about I buy you a cup of coffee at the Windmill Cafe?"

"I wouldn't have given you the knife if I didn't have somethin' else in my pocket."

Was he bluffing about having another weapon or telling the truth?

I waited.

"Okay," he said. "Let's have coffee."

At the Windmill Cafe we drank our coffee in silence. The young man's eyes had the same haunted look I'd seen in them before. I couldn't imagine the kinds of demons he faced. No wonder he was a loner.

"You wanted to talk about Star," I prodded after a while.

"Star was the only downtown kid who was nice to me." Arnold lit a cigarette, took a long drag. He held the cigarette between nicotine-stained fingers.

"Me and Star was gettin' to be, you know, boyfriend and girlfriend."

Star had told me that Arnold had misread her friendliness. When she pulled back from him, he threatened to hurt her. I wondered again whether Arnold was Star's killer.

When Arnold raised his eyes to meet mine, I felt a chill. He crushed out his cigarette and lit another. "She was okay even if she hooked up with that loser, Red Feather. I figured she'd realize Red Feather wasn't no good for her and we'd get together. Now that pig, Johnson, is saying bad stuff about Star. He's calling her a slut and a whore. But that fucking cop ain't gonna get away with bad-mouthing her. I'll make sure the son-of-a-bitch never says another bad thing about her."

Had he heard Johnson calling Star these names or heard someone else report it? Maybe he was imagining it. "I don't want you to get yourself in serious trouble," I said. "Just keep thinking good thoughts about Star and forget about Detective Johnson."

"You don't understand," he said, then resumed his sullen silence.

After a few minutes I said, "Arnold, do you have any idea who killed her?"

He took a deep drag on his cigarette and stared at the table.

I put a buck on the table for the waitress and stood up. "I'm going to the bathroom," I said and walked toward the restroom near the front door. Then I walked straight out of the restaurant, got in my car and drove home.

A short time later, feeling queasy, I sat on my living room couch, thankful to be safely back home.

Except, I'd just ditched a member of my street congregation. Would that come back to haunt me?

CHAPTER 7

"I can understand why you wear that collar, Robbie," Mother said, "even though it makes you look like one of those Roman Catholic priests." It was her day for childcare, and she stood at the kitchen sink drying the breakfast dishes. "Can't you at least wear a sport coat and slacks? Do you ever wear that nice tie I gave you? A minister has to project the right image. With that beard and long hair, you look like one of those hippies or gang kids yourself. Is that what you want?"

"Thanks for taking care of Andy, Mother." I said, ignoring the criticism, as usual.

She shook her head and scowled, then said, "Messiah Church in Pella, Iowa, is vacant. Your dad could suggest they consider you for a call."

"I'll think about it," I muttered.

I had awakened that morning knowing what I needed to do. I drove to the police station where I asked to see Detective Johnson.

The detective entered the lobby, wearing slacks with suspenders and a white shirt with sleeves rolled up. He tightened and straightened his tie. With a slight smirk, he said, "Reverend Vander Laan. To what do I owe the honor? Have you decided to quit coddling those punks?"

"I'd like to talk to you for a minute," I answered in a level tone.

He led me past the juvenile division, vice squad and interrogation rooms to his desk in the detective bureau. Kincaid sat at the next desk doing, paperwork. He looked up and greeted me. Johnson pointed toward a chair while he remained standing. It reminded me of the many times my father had made me sit while he stood and delivered a lecture.

"I'll stand, thanks," I said.

"Suit yourself. What've you got for me?"

"Information about a threat on your life."

His head jerked a fraction and his eyes narrowed. He pulled out a chair and sat down. "Please," he said, indicating the other chair.

I sat down and told him about my late night ride with Arnold.

"You think he's got a gun?"

"I don't know."

"You think he'll try something?"

I shrugged. "I just thought you should know so you can do whatever you need to do."

"You want to press charges on his threatening you?"

"No."

"Why'd you tell me? You guys usually try to hide behind that confidentiality thing."

"I woke up this morning knowing it was the right thing to do."

Johnson grunted. "Can you describe Arnold?"

I did.

"Got an address on him?"

I gave him the address where I picked Arnold up.

Kincaid slid his chair in my direction. "This Arnold frightens you, doesn't he?"

"Yes."

"Do you feel afraid of any of the other young people you work with?"

I shook my head.

Johnson stood up. "Could this guy have killed the Wynsma girl?"

I stood, too. "Maybe. I don't know. Arnold wanted Star to be his girlfriend. She told me he threatened to hurt her when she pulled back. When I asked him last night if he had any idea who killed her, he didn't answer."

"Okay. One more thing. Different subject. You were in the park with Peterson from the *Times* when a few of the uniforms were having a little chat with some of your punks. I never saw anything in the paper about that. You know why?"

"It was Stu's decision, but I did suggest it might be better not to make a big deal of it."

Johnson peered at me closely, then grunted.

* * *

Arnold showed up at the Ministry that evening, wearing the same heavy jacket he'd worn the previous night. Since two of the volunteers had to leave Drop-in early, I was covering it with Nathan and a volunteer. Rather than joining the other kids and me around the table, Arnold walked to the door of my office, leaned against the doorjamb, and stared at me.

As I walked to my office, I signaled Nathan, hoping he'd read my need for backup.

"Arnold," I said, gesturing for him to precede me. I took the chair behind my desk. I wanted something between Arnold and me.

He sat down, then got up and started to close the door.

"Leave it open. I'm covering Drop-in tonight."

He returned to his seat and stared at me. "You ditched me."

"That's right. I don't like being threatened with a weapon."

"Gimme my knife back."

"No."

"That's stealing."

I said nothing.

He patted his jacket pocket. Did I see a bulge there? "Gimme my knife back." he repeated louder this time.

I shook my head as Nathan appeared in the doorway.

"Oh, sorry, Rob. I see you're busy. I'll just wait here till you're free." He maintained his position in the doorway.

Good man, that Nathan.

Arnold stared at me another moment. "You squealed on me to Johnson."

"Threatening a police officer is serious business, Arnold. I did what I felt was necessary."

After looking at Nathan, Arnold got up without another word and left the building.

I briefly filled Nathan in on the situation and thanked him for his timely appearance before returning to the kids in the other room.

Shortly before closing time, Gimp disappeared to go to the bathroom and never returned.

After we shooed the rest of the kids out and locked up, Nathan turned to me. "Flushed himself down the toilet, you think?"

After a beer and a hamburger with Nathan at Mo's Bar and Grill around the corner, I was walking to my car to head for home, when Johnson pulled up to the curb. Kincaid rolled his window down and motioned me over. I crouched down by the window.

"We picked up this Arnold character and took him in for questioning," said Johnson. "He's a real whack job. Didn't have anything to hold him on, though, so we kicked him."

I told him about Arnold's visit to Drop-in.

Johnson scowled and shook his head. "Going on that late night ride with him was stupid. Don't do it again."

Concerned about my welfare? That would be a new wrinkle.

* * *

"What? Huh?"

Jackie shook my shoulder again, and I rolled over, opening one eye to look at the clock. Almost 8:30. I wasn't ready to wake up, and, since Jackie was off on Thursdays, I felt irritated.

She shook my shoulder more forcefully. "I just got a phone call. Some guy said there's a dead body in the back closet upstairs at the Ministry. I'd have thought it was a joke if it hadn't been for Star's murder."

I wanted to go back to sleep. Or maybe think about that church in Pella my mother had mentioned. Well, maybe not Pella, but there was still Washington Avenue. Even as the thought crossed my mind, I knew I couldn't leave the Street Ministry now.

I got out of bed. "Whose body?"

"He didn't say. Just hung up."

"Did the caller identify himself?"

"No. What the heck is going on, Rob?"

"I wish I knew. I'd better call the cops." I headed for the study. As I reached for the phone, it rang.

Lydia. Her voice was shaky. "I'm at the office. I came in early to do some typing and found the front door unlocked. I probably shouldn't have done it, but I looked through the whole building. My God, Rob! I found Cat's body in the back closet upstairs."

"Oh no! Not Cat." Outlaw's girl. "Jackie just got an anonymous phone call about it. I didn't know it was Cat."

"Anonymous? The killer, maybe? Or could it have been Gimp calling? He was probably sleeping here again." Lydia really was Communication Central.

"I'll be right down. You'd better call the cops."

"I just called them."

"You okay?"

"I feel like I lost another granddaughter." Lydia stifled a sob, and then I was listening to the dial tone.

I filled Jackie in on what Lydia had told me. She listened with her arms crossed, face neutral.

When I arrived at the Ministry, a uniformed officer was standing by the front steps, the door behind him propped open. I told him who I was, and he gestured for me to go inside. Lydia sat at the desk, red-eyed and blowing her nose.

I sat down next to the desk and took her hand.

At that moment she looked all of her seventy years. "Those two detectives are upstairs. Detective Johnson wants you to come up."

"You tell him about Gimp sleeping here?"

She shook her head.

I gave her hand a squeeze and then climbed to the second floor. At the rear of the building, I found Johnson squatting by the back stairs and looking down. Kincaid stood to the side, writing in his notebook.

Johnson stood with a grunt. "Lydia already I.D.ed the body, but why don't you step over to the closet here and take a look."

Cat's nude body was propped in a sitting position facing the open door of the closet. Her clothes were dumped in a pile next to her. Had she been raped? Her long red hair covered her face. I saw bruises on her neck. Johnson carefully pushed the hair away from her face. I confirmed that it was Cat.

There was no weakness in my knees, no nausea. Just a hard knot of anger in my belly. I looked away from the body to the rear stairs.

"Was she killed here or somewhere else and dragged up here?" I asked.

Johnson eyed me closely, but didn't answer.

I told him about the anonymous phone call.

"Any idea who it was?"

"The only person I can think of is a guy named Gimp." I explained about his recent sleeping in the building."

"You always let these delinquents sleep here?"

I mentally shuffled my feet. "No. And I guess we shouldn't have made an exception with Gimp. If he was the one who called, he was probably too scared to identify himself." I liked Gimp and my gut said he wasn't the murderer. Plus, he was a small man. Cat was tough and I expect she could have taken him.

"Can you give us a description of Mr. Gimp?" asked Kincaid.

"I assume Gimp's his nickname," I said. "He walks with a pronounced limp. Don't know his real name." I described him.

I wished I could talk to him before the cops picked him up. I wanted to encourage him to provide any information he could. It was part of the downtown code not to talk to cops. I suspected, however, that it would be easy for the cops to scare many of the kids into spilling their guts.

"Coroner's on his way," said Johnson, "and the evidence crew will be here any minute. You got somebody to vouch for you that you were home last night, or were you out doing your so-called ministry thing?"

"I got home about one. My wife will vouch for me."

"Is Cat her nickname," said Kincaid as he looked at the body. "And, if so, are you cognizant of her real identity or where her family resides?"

I shrugged. "Cat was Outlaw's girl. Lydia might know more."

Johnson shook his head. "What's with these stupid nicknames?"

He walked back down to the front office with me. "This building's sealed off as a crime scene until further notice. Staff can use their desk areas, but not your hangout rooms here or the back rooms upstairs. You'll need to fix the lock on the back door."

So someone had broken in at the back door. That would fit with Cat being killed somewhere else, dragged upstairs, and propped in the closet.

At Johnson's request, I said I would instruct Nathan and the volunteers to go to the station for fingerprinting and questioning. Lydia would go now, and I agreed to drop by the station later to answer more questions.

After Lydia left, I sat down at her desk and called Blaine, the former Ministry director. I told him about Cat.

"Johnson's been looking for an excuse to shut us down," I said. "I'm worried that he'll try to stall the reopening of Drop-In."

"Why don't I call the chief to see if I can make sure that doesn't happen?"

"I'm also worried the murders might jeopardize our support from the churches."

"I'll get the board president to call a meeting to deal with the churches. You need to put your energy into helping the kids cope with this."

Blaine's support made me feel like I wasn't facing this crisis alone. As I hung up the phone, I noticed Outlaw and Red Feather in front of the building, talking to the uniformed officer. Outlaw looked up at me.

"Cat never came home last night," he yelled through the open door. "And what the hell's goin' on here?"

I went down the steps and told the gang leaders about the discovery of Cat's body.

The color drained from Outlaw's face. He opened his mouth, but no words came out. He covered his eyes with his hand. Red Feather started to squeeze Outlaw's shoulder, but Outlaw shrugged him off.

I suggested that they go down to the police station to save Detective Johnson having to hunt them up. As they moved off, I doubted they'd take my advice.

With constant interruptions from various law enforcement people traipsing in and out of the building, I sat at Lydia's desk and tried to work on an upcoming sermon I'd be preaching in one of our supporting churches. I decided on a text from the Gospel of John, chapter eight, verse thirty-two. "The truth will set you free." I pulled out a tablet and made a few notes.

My mind, however, refused to stay focused on the sermon. I imagined Van Boven killing Cat and dragging her upstairs. Why kill her? Why bring her here? He probably didn't even know her. Then I pictured Arnold doing it. Same questions, though he knew Cat. Perhaps Outlaw was the murderer, but he seemed genuinely shocked and grieved. Of the primary suspects, he had the strongest connection to both victims. Maybe there was no relationship between the two murders, but that seemed unlikely.

Who else might kill two gang kids? I recalled Star's asking Deacon what he thought of Dirk. The kids frequently complained about his obscene and hostile comments to them. Of course, there were lots of folks who wanted the downtown kids run out of town, especially some of the nearby businessmen, but none of them would murder two young girls. Support the police crackdown on them, but not kill them.

My mind went back to my sermon. If I didn't get a new one written, I'd recycle an old one. That was the nice thing about preaching in different churches. I went to my office, put the tablet in a folder, wrote "truth/free" on it, and put it in the file drawer of my desk.

I heard Lydia returning from the police station. I headed back to her desk and sat down next to it. "How did it go?" I asked.

"All right. Not a lot I could tell them. I saw them bringing Gimp in while I was there."

"If you want to go home, I could cover the desk for you today."

She patted my hand. "Cat's real name was Lita Minor and she's from Allegan. I told Detective Johnson." She sighed. "What's happening here, Rob?"

"I don't know but it's really pissing me off."

CHAPTER 8

"**H**eard them punk kids are still killin' each other off," Dirk said, pushing up the visor of his baseball cap. "You got a dead one in the building, huh?" He looked over my left shoulder.

After replacing the lock on the back door and being interviewed at the police station, I'd grabbed lunch at Mo's Bar and Grill. Then I'd wandered over to the gas station next to the Ministry to see if Dirk or Harley witnessed anything the previous night that might shed light on Cat's murder. Dirk was there alone again, leaning on the counter and smoking a cigarette.

"Harley told me you guys sometimes play cards upstairs here after hours with friends. Did you notice anything suspicious around our building last night?"

"Nope," he said, gaze shifting to different parts of the floor. "Wasn't here."

As I walked into the Ministry, Lydia was taking a phone message for Nathan. When she hung up, I parked by her desk and we discussed the murders. "They're both Lost Souls and both females," she said. "Anybody got it in for the Souls that bad?"

We speculated for a while, getting nowhere.

As I stood up Lydia said, "I hear you're going to a rap session at Deacon's tonight. Could I go with you? Deacon said they'd probably get into some heavy theological stuff. He invited me to come. I miss the theological discussions I used to have with my late husband. Might help me take my mind off the murders."

"You bet," I said. "How about coming with me Friday night, too, for the whole night ministry shot? Think you could handle that, Granny?" It was something I'd been thinking about for a while.

"Thought you'd never ask," she said. Then, scowling, "But listen, buster, I'm am not your granny!"

Back in my office later, I pounded a fist on my Bible. I'd been staring at the words of John eight, verse thirty-two: "The truth will set you free."

What was the truth about Star and Cat? *God, please don't let any more kids be killed.*

I thought about Cat. Other than small talk, she never had much to say to me or to other staff, except for Lydia. I remembered the time I encountered Cat coming out of the bathroom at the Ministry. She had a black eye, and I asked about it.

"Bumped into a door," she said.

I gave her a skeptical look and said, "If you want to talk about what really happened, I'll be glad to listen. It would be confidential."

"No," she said. "It ain't nothin'."

I shook off thoughts of Cat and wrote several rough pages of notes on the sermon. Then I gave Lydia a hug on my way out.

"Don't worry about me," she said. "Just take care of the kids."

I spent half an hour walking downtown. I passed a theater and noticed on the marquis that *Midnight Cowboy* was showing. It was a film Jackie and I wanted to see. I watched people, the day-people who would be back in the suburbs before long. The night community was a whole different group, a unique parish: depressing, invigorating, freeing, compelling. It might be a strange congregation, but it was mine. And now two of my kids were dead. When I discovered Star's body, I wanted to run away. When I saw Cat's body, something in me hardened. Somebody seemed to think the street kids' lives didn't matter. How could I even consider leaving them now? I had to see this thing through. Washington Avenue Church was not in the cards for me.

Later, back in my office, I called the owner of Mo's Bar and Grill. I told Mo I wanted a meeting with some of the downtown businessmen, neighbors of the Street Ministry, to discuss their complaints regarding the kids and to talk about the murders. I didn't tell him that I also hoped to find out if any of the men had seen or heard anything related to the two killings. He offered to host the meeting at the restaurant. Neutral turf. I liked the idea. After setting it up for the next afternoon, I called and invited several area businessmen.

I said good-bye to Lydia and was heading for my car when Johnson pulled into the space behind it. I walked over and leaned down to the open passenger window.

"How about hopping in for a minute?" he asked, although it sounded more like an order.

I climbed in. "Where's Detective Kincaid?"

"Personal business. So what can you tell me about Outlaw and Cat?"

I thought for a moment about confidentiality and decided I'd never had a conversation with either of them that could be considered confidential. "Cat barely talked to me." I told him about the black eye episode.

"Outlaw give it to her?"

I noted that Johnson's tone with me was less hostile than before, still gruff, but more businesslike. "I don't know if Outlaw gave her the black eye. She never told me."

"She talk with anyone else on your staff?"

"Lydia," I said.

"Yeah. Lydia already talked to me." He cocked an eyebrow. Ever known Outlaw to be violent?" The sarcasm was back. Testing me, maybe?

"I broke up a couple of fights he was in or about to get into. He got busted for assault a little while back, but charges were dropped. Of course, you'd know about that. He has a quick temper, but Red Feather has been pretty good at reining him in since the Souls and the Night Stalkers merged."

Johnson looked surprised. "So that's the deal. Wondered why all of a sudden the Night Stalkers disappeared. Now, this Indian, he reins the other punks in?"

I nodded. "He pretty much tries to keep them on the straight and narrow."

"Why does Outlaw call you Chaplain?"

"When I was with the gangs at the merger meeting—"

"Hold up. You were at the meeting when they merged the gangs?"

"Yes. Someone made a crack about me being the gang chaplain. Then someone else made a motion and they voted me in as their chaplain."

"So you're a Lost Soul, too. Is that right, Reverend?"

I laughed. "I guess you could say that." I was thankful Stu Peterson, the reporter, wasn't listening.

Johnson's mouth looked like he had just tasted something sour. "Why did the gangs merge? I thought they were always at each other's throats."

"They decided to bury the hatchet, so to speak." I didn't want to say anything about how months of police harassment had resulted in dwindling numbers for both gangs. Several kids were in jail and others had left downtown. With gang numbers dropping, an uneasy truce had evolved and the idea of combining the gangs had gained momentum.

"So they buried the hatchet," Johnson said. "I'm surprised they kept the name of one of the gangs."

"That was Red Feather's work. The merger idea looked doomed until Red Feather urged members of both gangs to vote for him as vice president and Outlaw, leader of the Night Stalkers, as president of the new gang. Red Feather also suggested the merged gang be called the Lost Souls. That way each gang got something important."

Johnson shook his head. "Okay, Reverend, I'm sure we'll be in touch."

* * *

When Lydia and I arrived for the rap session, Deacon greeted us at the door and ushered us into the living room. Once again, I felt guilty, as if doing my ministry as usual diminished the importance of the most recent death. I pushed the thought from my mind and looked around. The room was furnished with a couch, two easy chairs, and several over-sized pillows scattered around the orange shag carpet. The walls were decorated with posters of rock groups, peace slogans and marijuana plants. Another poster showed the backs of four people—three men in suits and one young woman who wore a miniskirt and knee high boots—all lined up at urinals. The smell of incense added to the ambiance. The windows were open and a breeze cooled the apartment.

From the stereo came the sound of Simon and Garfunkle singing "Mrs. Robinson." A dozen young people lounged around the room, moved a little to the beat of the music and looked mellow. We knew most of the kids. Deacon introduced us to the two or three we didn't. Lydia and I sat on the only two straight chairs, near the door. I wondered if this was our host's little joke, seating the two straights on the straight chairs.

Deacon turned off the stereo, then said, "We'd planned to talk about the existence of God, but now with Cat's murder on top of Star's, some of us thought we needed to talk about that."

"Maybe the two subjects are connected," said Lydia. "If there is a God, how could he allow the girls to be murdered?"

"Right on!" said one of the kids. "That's exactly what I was saying."

With that, the discussion was off and running. I had a little trouble following some of the weird tangents, so different from the bull sessions I'd had with seminary classmates. Certain themes, however, seemed to recur. I pointed that out a couple of times, and then others would say things like, "Wow, there it is again. It's just like Rob said." And someone would point, as if the theme were visibly moving through the room. There would be general, good-natured laughter, which might have been at me.

As the discussion wound down, I asked if anyone in the room had an idea who might have killed the girls. One of them speculated that it might have been Arnold, but admitted the only basis for his suspicion was that Arnold was so strange. The question did get them talking about the girls and about their fears that the murderer might not be finished. What if the murderer started targeting heads as well as heavies?

When the meeting broke up, Deacon walked out of the apartment and into the hallway with Lydia and me. "Wanted to tell you," he said, "that I've got some ideas about Star and Cat's deaths. Just need to do a little more checking on some things."

"What are you talking about," I said. "Do you have an idea who did it?"

Deacon colored. "I'm not ready to say. What I'm wondering about may be stupid. Like I said, I need to do a little more checking."

I put a hand on Deacon's arm. "It doesn't matter if your ideas are stupid or far out. We've got to make sure there aren't any more murders. Maybe I can help you look into whatever you're suspicious of."

He looked at my hand on his arm.

"You're being awfully mysterious, Deacon," put in Lydia. "What's up?"

Deacon laughed nervously.

"Deacon!" The call came from inside the apartment.

"Gotta go," he said. "I'll get back to you."

"Wait, man," I said.

He backed up into his apartment and closed the door.

"What in the world was that about?" asked Lydia as we headed to my car.

"Haven't the foggiest. It reminds me that the night after Star was murdered and I was out with Stu Peterson, Deacon said something was bugging him about Star that he couldn't get a handle on. Maybe we should go back and demand that he tell us."

"I'm frustrated with him too, but he's got a good head on his shoulders. Let's give him a little time."

Later, as I drove her home, Lydia said, "The rap session was fun."

"But didn't you feel a little like the odd person out?"

Lydia laughed. "We were the only ones who weren't stoned."

"True. But how did *you* know they were high?"

"Deacon told me what to expect. I thought it was funny the way they'd go off on tangents, and the recurring themes thing was a hoot. You've never tried any drugs, have you, Rob?"

I shook my head.

"Me neither. I'm too old for that. Bet you'd like to try it though, wouldn't you?"

"Lydia, I'm a Calvinist," I said, putting on the most serious face I could muster. "I wouldn't do dope."

Smoking marijuana might be tempting in the right situation, but anything else seemed way too scary for me. I dropped Lydia off, then hit a few nightspots. When I got home, I fixed a piece of toast with peanut butter and jelly—comfort food. My mind kept returning to Lydia's asking me about doing dope. All I had to do was let Nathan know if I wanted to try marijuana. Nathan had lived for two years in the hippie community in San Francisco and was our resident drug expert. Maybe I should take him up on his invitation to join him for that music festival later in the summer somewhere in New York State. It might be the right opportunity to smoke a joint.

* * *

At noon the next day Lydia, Nathan and I met at Lydia's desk for a staff meeting. Mostly, we discussed the murders while we ate our lunches. Drop-in and the back of the building were still closed off as a crime scene.

We were nearly finished when Nathan proposed starting a drug help team.

"I think people can score drugs for themselves without your help," I said, raising an eyebrow.

"That's cute, but don't give up your day job. Or in your case, your night job. The team would help people who were having bad trips and get the word out about bad dope on the scene. We'd work closely with Rehab." Nathan referred to the new drug rehabilitation program the Ministry had helped create.

"How many would you want on the team?" asked Lydia.

"I'd like to train three or four to start and see how it goes."

I gave Nathan the green light. "Think Deacon would be worth considering for the team?"

"He'd be perfect," said Nathan. "I'll talk to him."

After the staff meeting, I went into my office to do some deskwork. When my phone buzzed, I picked it up and Lydia said, "Outlaw is here to see you."

"Send him in."

I'd debated about inviting Outlaw to the meeting with the businessmen to represent the street community. I'd be more comfortable with Red Feather, but I had to respect the gang structure. Outlaw had said he'd come.

When he entered my office, his face was drawn, making him look older, and his hair was long, but neatly combed. His jeans, black tee shirt and colors all looked clean.

"Hey, Chaplain," he said.

"Hey, Outlaw. You ready for the meeting with the businessmen?"

"Yeah. But maybe you better use my real name at the meeting. It's Lawton."

"Lawton it is."

"I figure I can wear my colors since you got yours on, right?" He pointed to my collar.

What could I say?

We walked past the gas station and around the corner to Mo's. Our host greeted us as we came in. We sat at a couple of tables pushed together in the back room. Harley Scanlon from the gas station, sat with his arms crossed. The owner of the furniture store on the other side of the Ministry knocked ash off a little plastic-tipped cigar. The owner of the jewelry store, directly across the street from our place, gave me a casual salute. Brandon Sharpe, owner of the camera store and one of my board members, smiled broadly. A moment later the manager of Sadie's Cafe walked in. I'd invited a few others, but they'd chosen not to attend.

Most of the men showed surprise or wariness as they looked at Outlaw. I said that Lawton, as president of the Lost Souls, was representing the gang and the other street kids.

Then I looked around at the faces of the men who had so much invested in their businesses and now felt threatened by the street people and by the murders. "Thanks for coming, gentlemen. We're all neighbors here in this part of down-town. There have been two murders which have, no doubt, had an impact on all of us. And it's no secret that some of you have been upset with the downtown kids. Lawton and I want to hear more about your concerns."

Harley scowled as he spoke. "I'm sick and tired of these characters hanging around my station. They park their jalop-ies in my customer spaces and cut through the gas pump area. The girls are nothing but whores, the way they let guys hang all over them. Now these hoodlums are killing each other. I've got customers who are afraid to come into the station when they see these guys in their stupid gang vest things. Lost Souls." He snorted. "At least they got that right. I think they should lock up every last one of 'em." He glared at Outlaw.

"Haven't you had some problems with the Ministry staff, too?" I said.

"Yeah," replied Harley. "You guys were parking in my customer spots, but that hasn't happened since we talked a couple of months ago. You being right next to us, it's like you're a magnet for the these street scum."

If I were in Harley's shoes, I thought, I would probably resent the kids, too.

"How about the kids cuttin' through your property and hangin' around the station? Is that still happenin'?" asked Outlaw.

"Not for the past week or so, but I expect it'll start up again."

Lawton just nodded. If he could learn the old nod, he might go far.

CHAPTER 9

"What problems are the rest of you experiencing?" I asked.

The jeweler said, "I've had a few people come in complaining that the kids were panhandling them. And I've heard a couple of comments about the, uh, public displays of affection. I have to say, though," he added, ever the diplomat, "the kids are never rude to me. I don't agree that they should all be locked up, Harley, although I can understand how you feel with the problems you've had. And, contrary to your assumption that the kids are killing each other, I don't believe the police know who murdered those girls."

Harley said nothing.

"I've had complaints about panhandling from some of my patrons, too," said the restaurant manager. "And these murders are making me real nervous."

Brandon Sharpe rubbed the back of his neck. "I really haven't had any problem except for a kid who stole a camera, and the cops arrested him. In fact, Red Feather… Oh, sorry. He's the vice president of the Lost Souls, Mr. Lawtons's right hand man." He winked at Outlaw. "Anyway, Red Feather came into my shop and apologized. Said it was one of his Lost Souls who did it, and he felt responsible." Brandon smiled at Outlaw who merely nodded. Brandon seemed to be implying great familiarity with the gang, a familiarity that he, in fact, did not have.

"I got the camera back," Brandon continued, "so I had the charges dropped. I think you all know I'm on the board of directors at the Street Ministry, so I wear two hats here. Personally, I think it's a great thing Rob is trying to do with those poor kids. The Street Ministry is our neighbor and we need to learn how to live with it."

I refrained from squirming at his reference to "those poor kids." Perhaps, too, Brandon really felt like he knew the gang because of his board connection and hearing my reports at meetings. Maybe I needed to cut him a little slack.

"Only real problem I had," said Mo, "was back when there were two gangs and there was a fight here. But, luckily, Rob was present and broke it up right away. The kids have been hanging out downtown for a few years, and they haven't hurt my business. I feel we need to give them a break. After all, they just lost two of their friends."

The furniture store owner hadn't said anything, and all eyes turned to him. He cleared his throat. "I'm the one who complained to the mayor after talking with a couple of you. I figured the kids would hurt my business. Can't say they have, though. Maybe I was a little hasty."

"Lawton," I said, "Think you could talk to the kids about the panhandling?"

"Yeah, I was thinkin' the same thing," he said. "I been trying to tell them that you guys got your own thing and we need to respect that. You all know who I am now, so if there's a problem, just talk to me."

"One more thing," I said. "Some of you might not have left work yet Wednesday night when the second gang member was murdered. Her body was found in a closet at the Ministry, though I don't think she was killed there. I'm wondering if anybody saw or heard anything that might be connected to her murder." I was thinking particularly of the restaurant guys.

"Business as usual here," said Mo.

"I was gone by a little after midnight," said the manager of Sadie's. "Didn't notice anything out of the ordinary."

The others said they were long gone.

I asked if anyone had anything else they wanted to bring up. No one did. I looked at Harley. "You may have a special situation being right next door to us with the station. Let's stay in touch on that."

He gave one quick nod.

I turned to the owner of the furniture store. "Any chance you might let the mayor know how we're dealing with the situation? The police have been coming down pretty hard on the kids for petty stuff."

He studied me for a moment, then said, "What do you mean, petty stuff?"

"This week three of the kids got ticketed for jaywalking, and one was arrested on a disorderly conduct charge for dangling his bare feet in the pool at the park. That kind of thing and worse has been going on for months."

"Okay, Rob, I'll talk to him."

"I'll talk to him, too," said the jeweler.

"I could put in a word," said Brandon. "I know the mayor pretty well."

Brandon Sharpe often referred to his political connections in the city, and I knew he was considering a run for a seat on the city commission.

"Might be better if you didn't, Brandon," I said. "The two hats you mentioned."

A dark look flashed in his eyes, quickly replaced by that broad smile. "You're probably right, Rob. I get too enthusiastic about the Ministry sometimes."

I'd seen that dark look of Brandon's before when I differed with him at board meetings. Another board member had warned me that Brandon hated it when people disagreed with him publicly. "You keep that up and there'll be payback time," the board member had said. He sounded like he was speaking from personal experience. Despite my questioning, the board member had refused to elaborate.

As we left, Brandon asked if I had a minute. Outlaw went on by himself, and I walked with Brandon to his store. He talked for a while about how great the kids were, how much he liked serving on the board, what a fantastic job I was doing. For some reason I always had trouble letting in his praise, though I had no complaints about his work as a board member. Then he said, "You know, I grew up poor. I think that's why I understand these kids."

Not all the street kids grew up poor, of course, but I said, "If you grew up poor, I imagine you're really happy your businesses are doing well."

"Oh yeah," he said, a look of fierce determination in his eyes. "I'll never be poor again."

Then he pressed me for details about finding Cat's body, but I told him Johnson didn't want me to talk about it.

"As a member of your board, I think I have the right—"

I was let off the hook when a fashionably dressed dark-haired woman walked up and gave Brandon a kiss on the cheek. She greeted me, looking at me through narrowed eyes.

I'd met Brandon's wife in the spring at a board reception. I had the same uneasy feeling now as I did then, that she was making a critical appraisal of me.

* * *

Lydia was sitting on her front porch swing when I arrived to pick her up for night ministry, and she hurried down the steps. I reached over to open the door, and she climbed in.

"How do you like my peace sign?" she asked as she pointed to the emblem hanging from her neck. "I got it at that head shop on my way home from work. I've never been there before, but Nathan told me about it. All kinds of drug paraphernalia, psychedelic posters, incense. That's quite a store."

"I've been there. You look pretty hip."

"Thanks. Let's hit the streets."

"Since we're on the West Side, I thought we'd start at the Corner Pocket. You ever shoot any pool?"

"My late husband had a table in the basement. I played a little."

When we entered the pool hall, I looked for Ronnie, a young pool hustler I sometimes ran into here. I didn't see him among those playing. Lydia and I chose a table. As I racked the balls, she handled a few of the cue sticks from the rack on the wall until she found one that suited her.

"Want to break?" I asked as I walked to the rack to find a stick.

"Okay. How about a game of eightball, and what say we put a buck on the game? Make it a little more interesting."

"No problem." Lydia could afford to lose a buck.

As I was turning back toward the table, I heard a solid crack. It was a clean break, balls scattering and two solids dropped into pockets.

"Wow, that was a lucky shot," said Lydia, beaming. "Now, let's see what we can do here."

I stood out of the way as she sank three more solids. There was no hesitation in her shots. Finally, she missed one, trying to sneak a ball past a stripe partially blocking a pocket. I noticed she hadn't tried for the shot that would have been easier.

I sank three stripes and missed my next shot.

Lydia moved around the table. Then she dispatched each of her solids in quick succession. She eyed the eightball, tapped the pocket to her right and popped the eight off the far side into the pocket.

She looked up and smiled. "What can I say? Beginner's luck."

Right. As I dug a bill out of my wallet and forked it over, I noticed a ten-dollar bill appear on the edge of the table. Lydia and I looked up together to see Ronnie standing with his cue stick, a smile on his face.

Lydia pushed my shoulder lightly. The message was clear: *Bug off, loser*. As the young shark racked the balls, Lydia placed a ten-dollar bill alongside his.

Lydia's break this time dropped three stripes and one solid. She didn't have a clear shot at anything. After walking around the table twice, she selected a shot at the ten, which was partially hidden. She cushioned off the rail, the ten narrowly missing the pocket. Ronnie quickly dumped four balls and then almost made an impossible shot.

After dropping three more stripes, Lydia missed a tough one. Ronnie finished off his solids and dumped the eight in the called pocket.

I reached into my pocket for a quarter. I always lost to Ronnie, and I always bet a quarter since he wouldn't play without a bet. The manager had told me that ten dollars was Ronnie's minimum bet, but for some reason he made an exception for me. Before I could cough up my measly two bits, Lydia laid another ten on the edge of the table. She racked the balls.

Ronnie sank five solids before turning the table over to Lydia. She cleaned house in one turn. I'd never seen that before.

Their last game was a close one, but Lydia was first to sink the eightball.

She introduced herself to Ronnie, and the two began chatting away like old friends. I didn't know if I was more in awe of Lydia's pool prowess or of her ability to engage

Ronnie in conversation. Even though we'd shot several games together, he never said much to me. I wandered over to chat with the manager, then returned.

"Rob, You should take some lessons from Lydia," said Ronnie. "By the way," he added, "I talked to Lydia about something that's been bugging me. She said she'd fill you in. Catch you later." He headed over to another table to talk with a guy shooting alone.

When Lydia and I returned to my car, I asked what was on Ronnie's mind.

"He said he shot pool a couple of weeks ago with an older guy who comes in once in a while. Ronnie said the guy was badmouthing gang kids, hippies and the Street Ministry, and he said that someone should eliminate them all."

"What's the guy's name?"

"Ronnie didn't know."

"Did you ask Ronnie what the guy looked like?"

"No. He seemed a little reticent, and I didn't push him."

"He say why he didn't tell me about this before?"

"I did ask him that. He said you remind him of his dad and he's a little uncomfortable talking to you. But then, he heard about the murders and he figured he'd better say something."

"We're going back in. Come on."

Back inside, we looked around for Ronnie. When we didn't spot him, I checked with the manager.

"Ronnie headed out the back door after you left," he said.

I hurried to the back door, which opened to an alley. Ronnie was nowhere in sight.

Returning to the manager, I asked if he remembered Ronnie shooting with an older guy who sometimes came in.

"Ronnie shoots with anyone who's willing to make a bet. I have no idea who you're asking about."

Lydia and I headed once more to my car. "Next time I see Ronnie," I said, "I'll ask him what this guy looked like."

I adjusted the rear view mirror. "Let's stop at River City so I can tell a waitress I know there about visiting her sister at the jail."

"Is that the visit you told me you were going to do the other day? What was her sister arrested for?"

"Yes, it's the visit I mentioned. Sam's sister was busted for soliciting."

When we got to the bar, I introduced Lydia to the bartender who was polishing glasses. Lydia and I each ordered a beer.

I saw Samantha waiting on a raucous bunch of guys at a booth near the pool table in the back. She soon came over, scowling, and set down a tray of empties.

"Looks like you're having a bad night," I said.

"It's those jerks in the back booth."

"Want me to go over and beat them up with my Bible?"

She punched my shoulder lightly. "Thanks for the offer, Rob. Seriously, though," she added, "did you bring your granny with you tonight for back-up? Afraid to face me alone?"

Lydia hooted, then introduced herself to Sam. "I'm happy to meet you, Sam. You're so pretty, it's no wonder Rob needs me for back-up."

Sam tossed her head back and flipped her hair with her hand. "Oh, shit, my order's up. Guess I have to go back to that table of jerks. She started to pick up her tray, then said to me. "Did you see Sis?"

"Yes, and I'm planning to go see her again next week."

"Thanks. I've been worried about her. I'm going to visit her tomorrow."

Sam headed away with her tray of drinks.

"I'm going over to watch the game at the pool table," said Lydia.

I stood at the bar, feeling lonely and awkward, an experience that was sometimes part of the job for me. Before the feeling could do more than register, the guy next to me struck up a conversation with the usual opener: What was a priest doing in a place like this? Several minutes later I glanced toward the back of the bar. The rowdy guys had quieted down. Could Lydia's presence nearby be the reason?

When Lydia and I left, I said, "I have to tell you that I'm pretty attracted to Sam."

"Of course you are. Is that a problem?"

"No. It's just that I encourage the volunteers to be open with each other about these things at our meetings, so I figured I'd better practice what I preach. What say we swing through the lot by Memorial Park and see if the Souls are around?"

At the park, two squad cars idled on the street. Four uniformed officers stood together, watching the park and the lot.

I pulled up to the curb behind them. As Lydia and I walked past them I said, "Good evening, officers. Hope you're having a good night."

One of the cops gave me a curt nod. The others ignored me.

Lydia wandered into the lot to talk with some of the Souls gathered there. I spotted the gang leaders sitting by the pool in Memorial Park across the street and headed there to join them. After we exchanged greetings I stood with my hands on my hips, studying the two young men. I could feel tension in the air.

"Outlaw wants to split," said Red Feather. "Thinks the cops will nail him for murder. I told him he's got to stick around." Red Feather looked at me, a plea in his eyes.

CHAPTER 10

Outlaw dragged his hand through the water of the shallow pool, a scowl on his face. "They think I did Star and Cat both. With my record, what chance I got if I don't split? Cat and me had a fight the night she was killed. I suspected her of gettin' chummy with Mad Dog. When she took off, Red Feather stopped me from going after her. Hell, I don't know what I'd a done if I did go after her then. I got people out of state I could stay with."

"Any idea who did murdered Cat?" I asked.

"That's the fuckin' trouble. I don't. Maybe Arnold. Good thing I don't know 'cause I'd probably kill the son of a bitch." Outlaw withdrew his hand from the water and dried it on his pants.

Perhaps he wanted to be talked out of leaving. "The cops will probably find you if you run. Can't anyone vouch for where you were after Cat took off?"

"Most of the gang saw me and Cat fightin' and saw me split later. I told 'em not to lie to the cops about it. I picked up a couple of six-packs, rode my bike out to the gravel pit. Got so shit-faced I passed out. Same as the night Star was murdered. Woke up this mornin' and went back to the pad."

"Okay," I said. "Hang in there. I'll stick by you."

"That don't mean lyin' for me. If the cops ask you any-thing about me, you tell 'em the truth."

"I will. You just have to stay around."

"I'll think about it," he said.

"And no more trips to the gravel pit by yourself to get wasted."

Red Feather looked relieved.

When I asked him about his grandmother, he bright-ened. "She's doin' a little better. I talked to her on the phone yesterday."

Crossing the river on Fulton, later, to avoid the circuit, I parked in the lot by a bar that was a fairly regular stop for me. Inside, I spotted a young man I'd met earlier in the sum-mer. I joined him and his friends at their table while Lydia went to talk with the bartender and another customer. I lis-tened to the guys at the table as they aired their complaints about their church.

When Lydia and I left the bar, I said, "It's almost one o'clock. Want me to buzz you home?"

"You trying to ditch me? The night's still young. You work later than this."

We moved on to the River City Hotel where we talked with three intoxicated conventioneers at the Lobby Bar in the hotel. After last call, we crossed the lobby and entered Sandy's Grill, which was filled with noisy patrons.

While we waited for our breakfasts, Lydia said, "I have to ask you something, Rob. Are you doing everything you can to stop these murders and find out who killed our kids?"

"I'm supporting the kids. I'm asking everybody I can think of if they have any idea who the murderer is. I'm pass-ing information and suspicions on to Detective Johnson. What else can I do? I'm not a cop. Are you trying to make me feel more guilty than I already do?"

"Of course not. You don't need any help in the guilt department from us Catholics. I just want you to think about the possibility that you may have better connections to get information than the police."

"I'll think about that."

I dropped Lydia off at three thirty. With her hand on the door handle she said, "This sure beats knitting in the wee hours when I can't sleep."

"I've really liked working with you the last two nights, Lydia."

"You like it enough to keep doing it?"

"Are you serious?"

"You bet. I have a niece who might be able to help at the front desk while we evaluate. She raised six kids and wants to do some volunteer work."

"Sounds great. If your niece is interested, bring her in next week and get her oriented. I may not be around Monday and Tuesday because Jackie and I are supposed to do that birthday getaway I told you about. I'm having second thoughts about going because of the murders. If we go, I'll meet your niece on Wednesday."

"I'll talk to Stacy tomorrow."

"Okay. See you tomorrow night, partner."

Was I doing everything I could to stop and solve the murders? Lydia's question gnawed at me as I drove home.

* * *

Over lunch Saturday, Jackie and I talked about our Grand Haven stay for my thirty-fourth birthday. I suggested postponing it because of the murders, but she wouldn't hear of it. We would stick with our plan to leave Sunday afternoon and return Tuesday, late afternoon.

With that settled, we got ready for visits to both our parents. We were ready to leave when Andy raced upstairs. A moment later we heard him slamming doors. I smiled. Jackie rolled her eyes. Andy had a ritual of closing all the interior doors before we left the house. We tried to discourage him, but our smiles and chuckles—mine, anyway—only encouraged him.

We arrived at Jackie's parents' farm near Borculo mid-afternoon. As soon as Andy got out of the car he raced to the fence by the barn to see Winston, Jackie's horse, and give him the carrot he'd taken along. Jackie and I joined Andy there, and Jackie rubbed the horse's neck. A moment later we walked toward the back door of the farmhouse.

The door was propped open, and Jackie's mom was sweeping out the entry room, which contained the new stairway to the basement. The original basement entry was from outside the house on the side by the driveway. Jackie's mom had demanded the basement be made accessible from inside. The old access was no longer used.

Jackie's mom put the broom in a cupboard and ushered us up the steps to the kitchen. I heard a radio announcer say, "This is WKYM, truly Christian radio." To a choral rendition of "Shall We Gather at the River," we paraded to the side porch where Jackie's dad sat reading.

"Hi, Grandpa," said Andy. "I brought a butterfly net. Daddy made it for me. Can we catch some butterflies in the yard?"

"Sure, Andy, that'd be great. Let me visit a little with your mom and dad, and then we'll see what we can find."

"Andy," Jackie's mom called from the kitchen. "Can you be my big helper and bring these cookies out to the porch?"

Andy raced into the kitchen, returning to set a plate of chocolate chip cookies, fresh from the oven, on the little table next to his grandpa's chair. Jackie's mom came to the porch with glasses of iced tea. We made small talk, avoiding discussion of the murders while Andy was with us.

After Andy and his grandpa did their little barnyard safari, I sat with my father-in-law in the lawn chairs under the big oak tree. He had purchased the farm when he'd taken the job as principal at a nearby Christian School. I'd always admired his keen mind, and I wanted his input regarding the murders. I ran down all the possible suspects—gang members, Arnold of the scary late night ride, Gimp who crashed at the Ministry, Star's neighbor who may have molested her, the guy who shot pool with Ronnie, and the guys from the gas station.

Jackie's dad peered at me closely. "You're a minister, not a detective."

"I know, but playing detective here in your yard can't hurt."

My father-in-law shot me a skeptical look. "Okay. First thing I'd say is don't rule anyone out because you like him or can't imagine him doing the murders. Or her, for that matter."

"I'll try to keep an open mind."

"Second thing may seem like a contradiction: What does your gut tell you?"

"That shortens my list considerably: first, the neighbor who sexually abused Star—whoever he is. Second, Arnold. Third, Harley or Dirk from the gas station."

"In that order of preference?"

I pondered that for a moment. "No. I can't rank them."

On the drive from Borculo to Holland, a short time later, Andy fell asleep in the back seat. We met my folks at a restaurant. The hostess ushered us to a table overlooking the water, and I took in the view of Lake Macatawa and the dark clouds that were building.

"So," said Mother, "another murder. I worry about you in that so-called ministry, Robbie. It's too dangerous. Have you thought about the Pella vacancy? The longer you stay with that Street Ministry, the more the good churches might think you're not suitable."

"Maybe I'm already not suitable, Mother."

"Nonsense. I'm just talking about what others might think."

"If you think I'd be a good match for the Pella church, you don't know me very well. Besides, I'm not ready to leave the Street Ministry after these murders. Do you have any idea how scared the kids are?"

Mother huffed.

At that point, Andy handed my mother the place mat he'd been coloring. "For you, Gram."

Good timing, Andy.

* * *

The thunderstorm hit as I drove home from Holland. Andy loved the lightning and squealed each time the thunder crashed.

When we got home, I read Andy a story, tucked him in and then changed into my clerical shirt and blue jeans. It had cooled off, so I put on a light jacket. I told Jackie that I planned to make it a relatively early night so we could go to church in the morning, since a friend and seminary classmate of mine was going to be the guest preacher. Then I headed to the West Side to pick up Lydia.

My street ministry partner came bouncing out the front door. She wore slacks, a plain white blouse and denim vest with flowered embroidery. "I talked to my niece, and she wants to volunteer at the front desk while we figure things out," Lydia said as she climbed into the car. "She'll come in with me Monday. You still planning to be in Grand Haven?"

"Yup. Jackie wouldn't be talked out of it."

I drove to Drop-In first, where Nathan and a few volunteers sat at the table with some straights from the suburbs and a couple of gang members. Nathan strummed his guitar.

Lydia sat down, and I was about to do the same when I got a call from Johnson. He wanted me to come to the station.

"Why do you want me to come down?" I asked.

"I have some more questions for you and some information about the body found at your place."

Lydia and I shoved off again. At the Hall of Justice, before the officer at the information desk could pick up the phone, Johnson walked into the lobby. He spotted Lydia and me and walked over. He asked Lydia to wait and motioned me to follow him as he headed back to the Detective Bureau. He indicated a chair and sat down behind his desk. I looked around the bureau. Two other detectives were at their desks, but I didn't see Kincaid.

"I'm holding Outlaw on suspicion of murder," Johnson finally said.

I backed up in my chair.

Johnson steepled his fingers. "All of a sudden Outlaw wants to be called Lawton. I'm thinking that there's bad blood between him and Red Feather. Lawton murders the Wynsma girl to get at Red Feather. We got some fresh prints off the closet door where we found Cat. Checking for a match with Lawton's prints now. We also found a knife on him, and we're checking it against the wounds on the Wynsma girl."

"You've arrested him for murder?"

"I didn't say that. We're holding him on suspicion. Haven't charged him. Yet."

I remained silent, wondering why he'd called me in.

Johnson stood, came around to the front of his desk and looked down at me with a scowl. I started to get up, but he placed a hand lightly on my shoulder. I sat back down.

"Here's my question for you, Reverend," he said. "You ever witness any hostility between Lawton and Red Feather? Or ever hear about any? And no confidentiality bullshit."

I hesitated. Johnson leaned closer, eyes narrowed. I don't respond well to intimidation. Never have. But I didn't want to be stupid either. I crossed my arms. If I told him that Outlaw had argued with Red Feather the night Star was murdered … But maybe he already knew that from some of the Souls. Shit!

The phone on Johnson's desk rang. He reached back and snatched the receiver, keeping his gaze on me. "Yeah." He listened a moment, then grunted an acknowledgement. He hung up the phone. "Now answer my question."

"Outlaw told me he argued with Red Feather the night Star was murdered and the night Cat was murdered."

"About what?"

"The night Star was murdered, he said they argued about a new kid in the gang. Outlaw wanted to kick him out, but Red Feather said the new kid needed the gang. The night Cat was killed, he said he was jealous because he thought Cat had been flirting with Mad Dog. Red Feather kept him from going after Cat when she left the pad." Even though Lawton had told me to tell the truth to the cops, I felt like a slimeball. Maybe I should have shut up and taken the consequences.

Johnson sat for a moment with his arms crossed, then said. "Anyways, just found out Lawton's prints don't match and neither does his knife. This doesn't mean he's off the hook, but I got no reason to keep him locked up. Want to go to holding with me to spring him?"

Once again I was caught off balance. I nodded dumbly.

I followed Johnson to the lockup. Three males, including Outlaw, were in one of the cells. Johnson looked at the guard and jerked his thumb toward the cell. The guard unlocked the door.

"Lawton, you're free to go," said Johnson. "Just stick around town in case we have more questions. Look who I brought to see you."

Outlaw looked at me with obvious relief. "Hey, Chaplain."

On our way to the lobby I reported what I'd told Johnson. "That's cool," he said. "I told him all that, too."

When we reached the lobby, Lydia looked at Lawton in surprise. He explained to her that he'd been picked up and released.

I offered to drop Outlaw at the Ministry. After he was settled in the back seat of my car, he said, "I was tryin' to find you guys when I got picked up and brought to the cop shop."

"What's on your mind?" I asked.

"Got into a hassle with Mad Dog last night. He wanted to bust into a place to get money to fix his car. I told him to get a job. He said I was gettin' so straight I'd probably rat him out if he ripped a place off. I split on my bike so I wouldn't hit him. Things have been gettin' to me more since Cat …" He paused and swallowed. "Anyway, thought I'd pick up a couple of six-packs and get shit faced. Then I remembered some guy in a white collar tellin' me that wasn't a good idea."

My gaze met Outlaw's in the rearview mirror.

"So I cruised on my bike for a while. About two this morning, I drove through the alley behind the Ministry. I saw some guy pokin' around by the back door. I pulled up and asked what the hell he was doin'. He turned around and I seen it was Arnold. I ain't got no use for him, but he's so wacko, I don't want to cross him neither."

"What did he say?"

"He said it was none of my business what he was doin' and walked off toward the park. Figured I should tell you."

"I'll pass the information on to Johnson."

"Another thing … Would you guys mind calling me Lawton instead of Outlaw. Just seems, I don't know, maybe I've outgrown … I'd just rather …"

"Lawton," I said, glancing at Lydia. "I'll try to remember."

"Lawton it is," said Lydia.

"By the way," I said, "you did well at the meeting with the business guys."

* * *

After church the next morning, we dropped Andy off at the farm, and Jackie and I headed to Lake Michigan. The two days at the beach in Grand Haven exceeded my expectations. The weather, the food, the lovemaking—all were perfect. It was one of those falling-in-love-all-over-again times. The frosting on my birthday cake, so to speak, was watching the news of Neil Armstrong's walk on the moon.

When we got back to Borculo Andy rushed outside to meet us, carrying a jar with two butterflies, the jar's lid punctured to allow air inside. "This one's a Black Swallowtail, Daddy," said Andy proudly, pointing to the black butterfly with yellow spots. "And this one is a Great Spangled Frit— um, Fri–till–a–ry." He pointed to the orange one with brown marks on the top and silver spots on the bottom.

"Wow, Andy," I said. "I'm very impressed." Jackie's dad had taught high school biology before taking the job as principal. Sounded like Andy might be catching his grandpa's love of nature.

"Guess what, Daddy? There really is a man on the moon. I want to go to the moon when I get big." Andy had seen the TV coverage too.

Back in Grand Rapids, Jackie and I spent a quiet evening at home playing with Andy and freeing the butterflies.

I was drifting off to sleep when I realized I'd hardly thought about the murders for almost two days. Suddenly I was wide-awake, dreading my return to work. Lydia's question reverberated in my head: Was I doing everything I could to stop and solve the murders?

CHAPTER 11

Robbie, I just heard that Pella is calling Bill Den Besten. Wasn't he a classmate of yours? I know his dad was a minister in Zeeland when we were in Sioux Center." Mother was gathering up the dishes from lunch as Andy dashed out the back door for the sandbox.

"Yes, we graduated together. I think Bill should do well in Pella."

"That's what happens when you wait too long. Now Pella's not a possibility, unless Bill declines." She ran water into the sink.

"I'm pretty happy where I am."

"It doesn't hurt to keep your options open," she said sharply. Then, in a more conciliatory tone, "I hear the Jamestown church will soon be vacant. If you were in Jamestown, you'd be close to Grand Rapids and important contacts in the denomination. Jackie could keep her job. Jamestown's a nice church. At least, that's what your father says."

"Any church can extend a call to me anytime it wants to, Mother," I said, my voice raised a notch. "But I'm not ready to leave the Street Ministry, and I want you to stop bugging me about it."

Mother turned around slowly to look at me, but didn't say anything. I thought about apologizing but didn't. I'd said what I wanted to say for months. Maybe I could learn something from my mother and Jackie about speaking my mind and letting the chips fall where they may. I used to do that all the time, often getting into trouble for it. But sometime in high school I'd cleaned up my act, and now I was beginning to question that.

At the Ministry later, I found Lydia and her niece at the front desk. "Stacy is catching on quickly," said Lydia.

"Nice to meet you, Stacy," I said. "I'm sure Lydia has told you that our receptionist situation is in limbo until we decide if she will keep doing night ministry with me."

Stacy flashed a friendly smile. "Yup, Aunt Lydia told me, and I'm flexible for now. I'm just happy to have some work."

We talked for a while about the moonwalk, and I answered some of Stacy's questions about the Ministry. "You should know," I said "the real expert on the Ministry is your aunt. She's been here from the beginning, and she even knows everything we don't want her to know. It's why we call her Communication Central."

"I know I've got big shoes to fill," said Stacy, grinning at Lydia.

Lydia snorted and shook here head.

"Good thing I've got big feet, right Aunt Lydia?"

At that Lydia laughed and said, "She's right about that, Rob. I called her Bigfoot when she was a teenager."

My first impression of Stacy was positive—a woman who radiated warmth and confidence.

As I sat in my office later, I thought about Warren Van Boven, Star's neighbor. He wasn't on my short list of murder suspects because I knew so little about him. But if he was the neighbor who abused Star and she was about to blow the whistle on him, he'd have motive to kill her. According to Red Feather, the neighbor who molested Star patronized prostitutes on South Division. I wished I were acquainted with some of the women who worked the street. I'd said hello to a few on my night ministry rounds, but I'd been mostly ignored. Except for one who wanted to know if I was interested in doing a little business. Maybe they knew something or could find out something. I did know Sam's sister, but she was in jail.

Of course, maybe Red Feather had made up the story about Star's neighbor. But even if he had, which I doubted, I had nothing to lose by asking Sam's sister if she knew Van Boven.

That's the cops' job, not yours," said a voice in my head that sounded like my mother.

Then Lydia's voice echoed in my mind: *You may have better connections for information that the police..*

Twenty minutes later, I was at the county jail in the visitors' room, struck again by how similar Sam and her sister looked.

"Hi, Rob. Didn't expect to see you so soon."

"How you doing?"

"Same shit, different day. How about you?"

"I'm good. Has Sam been in to see you?"

"Yeah. She came in the day after you did."

We made some more small talk, and then I said, "Do you remember that when I came to see you before, we talked about Star's death?"

"The girl you found murdered. I remember."

"Somebody told me she had a neighbor who was forcing her to have sex with him."

"Think he murdered her?"

"Possibly. I'm told this guy picks up women on South Division." I decided I had nothing to lose by describing Van Boven. "He's in his forties, flaming red hair, face severely pockmarked."

"Sounds like a guy I partied with a couple of times, but he usually likes to party with Dolores, a black hooker. *If* it's the same guy."

Sometimes it pays to play a long shot. "If I wanted to talk to Dolores, how would I go about it?"

"She wouldn't talk to you. If I was out, I could introduce you and she might talk. Hey, are you friendly with any hookers besides me?" she asked with a spark in her eyes and a grin that reminded me of Sam.

I smiled and shook my head.

"Two weeks and I'm out. I could introduce you to Dolores then."

Shit. Two weeks was a long time.

"Oh, hey, Sam could introduce you."

"Really? How does Sam know Dolores?"

"Sam worked the street for a little… Oops. I don't think she wanted me to tell you that."

I was shocked but tried not to show it. "I'll speak with Sam."

"Still doubt Dolores will talk, though."

* * *

"You and Jackie are going to look good in the paper tomorrow next to that "Make Love Not War" poster," Lydia said.

I blew through my lips and waved a hand dismissively. "I expect they'll find more interesting photos to print." To be honest, I was afraid she might be right because of my collar.

Along with Jackie, Nathan and most of the heads we knew, Lydia and I had participated in the early evening anti-war demonstration. Now, after dropping Jackie at home,

Lydia and I were heading back downtown and discussing the event.

"Lots of police around, weren't there?" she said.

"At least the cops weren't bashing heads or using tear gas."

"Yes, I worried a little about that."

Then I told Lydia about visiting Sam's sister at the jail and her saying that Sam might introduce me to Dolores.

"Sam knows this Dolores?"

"I wondered about that, too. Apparently Sam worked the street for a while."

Lydia was quiet for a moment, a look of pain in her eyes. Then she said, "Seems like a long shot to try to get something on Star's neighbor with Dolores's help."

"So was describing Van Boven to Sam's sister. If there's a chance that Delores could help us find out if he's the guy who killed Star—"

"You've got a family to think about. It might be dangerous."

"Hey, you're the one who's been bugging me to do something. What's with the negativity? If you want to bail, I can drop you off at home, or I can bring you to Drop-in."

As we pulled into a parking spot near the River City Hotel, Lydia said, "You're right. It's worth a try."

Things were quiet at River City Lounge.

"Looks like a slow night," I said to Sam when she came to the bar.

"Yeah, real slow."

We sat down at a nearby table. "I went to the jail to see your sister again today," I said.

Sam brightened.

I told her about my visit. "Your sister says if you do the intro's, there's a chance Dolores will talk to me."

"Sis tell you how Dolores and I know each other?"

"She didn't really say exactly."

"Rob, you're a terrible liar. She told you I worked the street."

I nodded.

She turned to Lydia. "We have to teach this guy how to lie better." Then she added, "Seriously, I can guess what you two think of me now."

"If anything," I said, "you've gone up a notch in my estimation. You got yourself off the street. That had to take some doing."

Her eyes misted. Lydia put an arm around her.

Sam rubbed her nose then swiped the back of her hand across her eyes. It's so slow, maybe I can leave. My boss respects what you guys do, and he was upset about the murders. This is real important to you, isn't it, Rob?"

"It is."

"Let me talk to the boss."

As Sam walked to the bar, Lydia grinned at me. "Honestly, Rob, if Sam can do this right now, I've got to believe that *somebody* up there is looking out for you."

Twenty minutes later the three of us boarded Night Watch. Sam had changed into jeans and a pink blouse.

"It'll be tough to get Dolores to open up with you, Rob," said Sam, "but our best bet is to see her without Lydia." She looked at my ministry partner. "Sorry, Lydia."

Lydia scowled, but agreed. I dropped her off at the Ministry. If I wasn't back when Drop-in closed, Nathan would bring her home.

I cruised slowly down South Division with Sam. A car followed us. It looked like mine, except for the lack of artwork. Obviously, Vice Squad. I turned, circled the block and headed back up Division with Vice still on my tail.

"Dolores used to hang out in front of Amigos or the Alibi, said Sam." The former was on our left, the latter on our right a little further up.

At Sam's suggestion, I parked, and we scouted out the nearby bars and restaurants in a three-block area with no luck. Finally, we returned to the Alibi.

The waitress brought us each a draft. Sam wrapped her hands around the glass, then said, "Feels kind of weird to be wandering this neighborhood again." She had a look in her eyes I couldn't put a name to. "Glad those days are over."

I felt restless.

Sam studied me a moment. "You're squirming like you've got ants in your pants and you're playing with your beard. What's bugging you?"

"This whole thing is making me nervous."

"Why?"

"I really appreciate your help, Sam, but I'm not very comfortable about the whole idea of snooping into Star's murder. I should leave it to the cops."

"Knowing you, you'd feel rotten if you didn't do something."

Just then, a black woman walked in the back door. She wore a dark mini skirt and white blouse with the top three buttons open. Her skin was very dark, her hair dyed blond and straightened. Her face was attractive but hard. She spotted Sam, stopped in her tracks and grinned. Then she must have noticed my collar because she did a double take. She walked to our table and sat down, ignoring me. "Hey, Sam, how ya doin'?"

"Good, Dolores. How about you? Your man treating you okay?"

"Pretty good so far this week. You ain't back to workin' the street, are you?"

"I work at River City Lounge."

"Hey, you really cleaned up your act."

"I even started a class at Junior College."

"No shit. That's cool. You ain't gonna get too good to talk to me, are you, girl?"

"No way."

"So what you doin' here? It's been a while." Dolores glanced at me.

Sam introduced me to Dolores. "Rob is with the Street Ministry."

"Yeah?" said Dolores. "I seen him on the street a few times. But you ain't answered my question."

Sam told Dolores about Star's murder. Then Sam said that I had visited her sister at the jail and that her sister had said Dolores might be able to help.

"Me?" said Dolores "How the fuck can I help."

"I want to know about a guy who may be a customer of yours," I said. "He's in his forties, red hair, and his face is pockmarked."

"If he's my john, why should I talk to you about him?"

I told Dolores about finding Star's body and that this neighbor of Star's may have molested her. Then I said, "Star told her boyfriend that the neighbor guy wanted to pick up a woman he knew who works the street so the three of them could party together. That's when Star threatened to rat him out."

"A woman who works the street? Why don't you say whore, Reverend?"

"I didn't want to offend you."

"Well now, ain't that sweet? I'm a whore, Reverend. That's what I do."

After a moment I said, "This guy may have murdered Star."

"So why you talkin' to me 'stead of the cops?"

"I figured you wouldn't want the cops questioning you."

"You got that right. But why should I talk to you? You say you know Sam's sister, and Sam says you're okay. But I don't know you and that collar don't mean shit to me."

"I'm sorry I bothered you." I started to get up to leave. Reverse psychology, but I doubted it would work.

"Come outside," said Dolores. "Too many ears in here."

Sam and I followed her out the front door. Dolores stood looking down the street, hands on her hips. Considering? When she didn't say anything, I reached for my pocket. "I can see why you wouldn't trust me. Let me pay you something for your time."

"Don't look now, but that car parked across the street is Vice. Unless you even stupider than you look, you know what they gonna think if you be givin' me money."

"They've been following me since I hit the street."

A hint of a smile. "Now you know what I have to put up with."

"Dolores," I said, "may I give you a hug?"

"A hug!" She snorted. "What you wanna give me a hug for with Vice sittin' across the street?"

"Because I really appreciate your time."

She flashed me a skeptical look.

"I also think it's safer than giving those guys across the street the finger."

Dolores laughed and threw her arms around me.

Then she turned to Sam. "I'm startin' to see why you like this guy."

Sam laughed and grabbed my hand. "I trust him, even if he is a little uptight in the sex department."

"Maybe the three of us should go to my crib and help him lighten up."

Sam laughed. "He really is a good guy, Dolores."

"So what you wanna know about my john?"

"Warren is a customer of yours?"

"He calls hisself Charlie, but mostly they don't gimme their real names. I see him about twice a month on Friday nights."

I felt a jolt of excitement. "He's a regular customer, then?"

"Guess you could say that. Nothing too regular in this business, but Charlie's about as regular as they come."

"Is he ever violent? Think he could murder someone?"

"He ain't never been rough with me, but, hell, we all got that violence in us. But even if this Charlie/Warren guy did kill the girl, I still don't get what you want from me."

I had a half–baked idea Dolores could get Van Boven to admit he murdered Star. But even if he did, then what? Suppose it got as far as going to trial. The defendant would be Warren Van Boven, an upstanding, middleclass, church-going, white guy whom Star's parents liked. One witness for the prosecution would be a black prostitute, another, a gang member, part Indian, testifying that Star told him Warren had molested her and that she had threatened to rat him out. And wasn't it all the kind of thing that was dismissed as hearsay on lawyer TV shows? I never should have come to talk to Dolores.

"It sounds really stupid to me now," I said, "but I kind of thought maybe you could sort of get him to talk about it and, I don't know …"

The hard look was gone from her eyes.

"Let's think about it," she said. "Problem is I'd make a shitty witness. Tape recorder? No. Only two outlets in the room at my pad and Charlie would catch me turning it on. Somebody else would have to hear it, too. Not a cop, that's for damn sure. Somebody like you would have to hear it, maybe. Yeah, you could do it."

"Me? Are you nuts?"

"This was your fuckin' idea, remember?" The hard look returned to her eyes.

"I'm sorry, Dolores, but no way could I do that."

"Look, I expect he'll show Friday night. Too noisy in the bar on weekends to hear much of anything. Lemme see. He usually parks out back, and I could catch him there. You could hide behind the trash bin. Now, how do I keep him out there and get him talkin'?" She slipped a hand under her blouse and adjusted a bra strap. "If Sam was with me

and he thought there might be a three-way party for him …
yeah, that might work. He's usually a blabbermouth, and
he's always braggin' 'bout stuff. I got a good feelin' about
this, Reverend, even though I hate to lose a John."

A few minutes later, Sam and I sat in my car. "It could
work," she said. "I can get one of the other girls to cover for
me at the bar."

She slid over and kissed me lightly on the cheek. "If
you're not going to get us a room, maybe you'd better drop
me back at work." She looked at the clock on the dash.

The softness of her breast against my arm was electric.
As I turned to give her a peck on the cheek, she turned, too.
Our lips met and, for a moment, our tongues danced together.

I pulled away. "That probably wasn't a good idea," I said,
my heart pounding and my lungs unable to get enough air.

Sam looked serious. "I know. But that was *not* a one-way
kiss."

"Agreed."

I started the car, and Sam slid back to her side of the seat.
When we arrived at River City, I said, "Hey, what class are
you taking at J.C.?"

"English."

"Good for you."

Twenty minutes later, Lydia eyed me carefully as we
waited at Windmill Cafe for our coffee to arrive. "Tell me
what happened," she demanded.

After the waitress poured the coffee, I filled Lydia in on
the plan.

Her eyes lit up. "I'll skip my family reunion and eavesdrop with you."

"I'm sorry, but you can't. It's too risky."

Her face darkened. "I wonder if you should talk to
Detective Johnson."

"No. He'll put the kibosh on the whole thing or want a
cop there."

She sighed. "You're right."

"I'm not even sure it's worth the effort. Even if Van Boven admitted killing Star, he could just deny it or claim he was making it up to impress Dolores and Sam. But I can't think of anything else to do, and I have to do something."

After dropping Lydia off and driving home, I plopped on the living room couch, pulled off my collar and slipped it in the pocket of my shirt. I kicked my shoes off and sat there for a long time. I prayed. I worried. I lusted.

CHAPTER 12

I woke up feeling depressed, anxious and guilty. After breakfast, Andy and I shopped for groceries. By the time we got back home, he was coughing and sneezing with a summer cold. While Jackie heated chicken noodle soup for lunch, I read with Andy. He was sounding out some of the words now, thanks to his time with Jackie's mom. I felt much better after hanging out with him.

By early afternoon, I was in a meeting room in the River City hotel for my monthly report to the Urban Mission Committee, the arm of my denomination that supervised my work at the Street Ministry. Reporting to both my denominational committee and to the board of the Street Ministry might have been a little weird, except that neither tried to tell me what to do. After an initial period of feeling like the committee was looking over my shoulder with suspicion, I now felt supported by the members and looked forward to the meetings.

The men had completed their agenda except for my report. I was surprised to see John Vanden Berg, the minister from Star's family's church.

The committee chairman tamped down the tobacco in his pipe and said, "Rob, I think you know John. He was asked to serve on the committee."

John and I shook hands.

Another committee member, an insurance agent from Grandville, asked, "How are you doing with the murders, Rob?"

"I guess I'm doing okay. I've got people I'm talking to about it."

"Are the police making progress in the investigation?" he asked.

"If they are, I don't know about it."

After I reported on my work for the past month, the chairman asked if there were any questions.

John cleared his throat and looked ministerial. "Rob, do you talk to these people about God and getting their lives right with Him? After all, that's what mission is about, isn't it?"

That was typical of John. It wasn't his question that frosted me so much as his asking it in his first meeting, his assumption that he already knew more than I did about my ministry.

I explained to him that the Street Ministry wasn't there to judge or criticize people. We were there to build bridges of understanding and acceptance between the alienated and the Church. I pointed out that many of the people I ministered to had been hurt by the Church. As I looked at John, I knew what I'd said was as welcome as a fart in the middle of his sermon.

Another committee member, a banker, came to my rescue. "But Rob," he said, "you've told us before that you do sometimes talk about God and spiritual things with the street people, isn't that right? You've even had Bible studies with some of them."

"That's true. Many of them are very interested in religious and spiritual questions and grew up in a church. I usually wait for them to bring the issues up."

"Another question, Rob," said John. He spoke in a deep, resonant baritone, the voice of God, evoking awe, perhaps fear in most people. He was a little over six feet tall, and his voice gave him a commanding presence. It also made him a very popular preacher. "You're spending time with all these people who are into drinking and drugs and promiscuous sex. How do you keep yourself from falling into temptation?"

"I pray and I talk openly with my wife and my colleagues at the Street Ministry about the temptations. You know, there are drinking and drugs and sex outside of marriage going on among some of your church members, too. I've talked to a few in my work. How do *you* keep yourself from falling into temptation?"

John reddened. "Tell me who you've talked to. I'm their pastor. I have the right to know."

"No, John. I can't tell you things shared in confidence. It would destroy my credibility and the credibility of the Street Ministry. I'm sure you understand."

"I think that's enough for today," said the chairman. "Rob needs to get back to work, and we all need to do the same."

At the chairman's request, the banker offered a prayer for my family and me, for the Street Ministry, and for God's protection over the kids I worked with. He prayed for the families of Star and Cat. I felt touched and cared for.

After the meeting, instead of heading straight back to my office, I walked downtown for a while. I asked God to forgive me for my intolerance of judgmental people. I soaked up the words of the banker's prayer. I prayed for John. *What a sanctimonious prick*, I thought, hoping that wouldn't cancel out my prayer for him.

I was quite sure I'd not heard the last from him.

When I returned to the Ministry, Sid Johnson was coming down the front steps. He stopped on the sidewalk.

"What brings you here?" I asked.

"Had to see Lydia. Gave her a note we found in the shirt pocket of the dead girl in your closet. By the way, Reverend

Vander Laan," he added, "what were you doing on South Division hanging out with the whores?"

"My job," I said. I wasn't surprised that he'd been informed of my presence there by the Vice cops who worked the area.

"Is a public display of affection with hookers part of your job too?"

"Sometimes."

"I guess you're just a loving kind of guy, huh?"

I said nothing, and Johnson moved off toward his car.

When I entered the building I found Lydia in tears. I sat down in the chair beside her desk and put my hand on her shoulder.

She passed me a piece of paper. "Detective Johnson found a note in Cat's pocket and made a copy for me."

I read it silently.

Dear Lydia
I never knew my Gramma but if I had one I'd want her to be just like you. I know you get mad sometimes when us kids call you Granny but it shows how much we like you.
Love Cat

I hugged Lydia while she sniffled into my shoulder. After a moment she blew her nose. "I just hope they catch the no good so-and-so who killed her."

"Me too." Then, changing the subject, I asked, "How's Stacy doing?"

"She's doing fine. She'll be able to work mornings for the rest of the summer. I think she'll be ready to be on her own next week, and I won't have to come in till early afternoon. I can hang out with you till the wee hours."

"Great, partner."

"Don't forget, though, that tonight I'm visiting with friends from out of town. And tomorrow I've got my family reunion."

I headed to my office to do some more work on that upcoming sermon. As soon as I sat down, my mind went to the murders. I thought again about Arnold. Maybe he was capable of murder. I thought about Van Boven, Star's neighbor. He might have had a motive to kill Star, but why Cat?

I had serious reservations about hiding behind the trash container in back of the Alibi. I could tell Dolores I'd changed my mind and decided to leave solving the case to the police. But I was kidding myself. I was the one with the connection to Dolores. I had to follow through, come what may.

As I leaned back in my desk chair, my mind turned to my attraction to Sam. I knew what I'd do. I'd visit River City with Jackie sometime and introduce the two of them. That should help cool things with Sam. In fact, now that I'd broken the dance barrier, I could boogie there with Jackie.

Back to my sermon: "The truth will set you free." I wrote a couple of pages of notes and put them in the folder.

I was about to leave when Lydia stuck her head in my office and said, "Phone call from your Urban Mission Committee chairman."

I grabbed the phone. "What's up?"

"We met for another half hour after you left. John was upset. He thinks the committee should thoroughly examine your theology with you. I told him that was inappropriate and I wouldn't support it."

"Okay."

"You could have been a little more diplomatic in your answers to his questions. If he raises enough of a stink the matter could go to Synod, which, as you very well know, has the power to kick you out of the ministry."

"How did the meeting end?"

"I encouraged John to take time to get to know your work. I said the committee needs to focus on supporting you through this murder business. John agreed not to do anything before our meeting in September."

That son of a bitch.

* * *

"If you'll come with me to the bar and let me introduce you to Sam," I said to Jackie, "it could diffuse the attraction. What do you think?"

While Andy played with a neighbor kid a couple of houses down, I sat with Jackie in the living room where I'd told her about Sam and my attraction to her.

Jackie glanced at me and then looked back to her knitting. "With Lydia as your night ministry partner, Sam being a turn-on for you shouldn't be a problem. Talk with Lydia about it."

"I already have, but she might not always be with me. I just want to err on the safe side."

Jackie continued knitting, but peered at me more closely while I feigned a nonchalance I didn't feel.

"Is the River City a dive?" she asked.

"It's a decent bar, although the waitresses wear sexy outfits." I thought she should be prepared. "Besides, we could dance."

At that she dropped her knitting and squinted at me. "You don't dance."

"Sam ambushed me the other night and dragged me onto the dance floor. So I guess I can dance. But I'd rather dance with you."

Jackie's knitting fell to the floor as she leaped onto my lap and gave me a kiss and a hug. She had fallen in love with dancing when she spent a year overseas, living with a cousin in Amsterdam. She'd long ago given up trying to get me to dance with her. "Okay," she said, unable to refuse my bribe. "Tomorrow night. You can start your rounds a little late."

I thought about the plan to eavesdrop behind the dumpster. "Tomorrow night's not the best time."

"Why not? Lydia's not going with you." She gave me her squint-eyed look again. "You sure you want me to meet this Sam?"

I thought about that *accidental* kiss. "Tomorrow night," I agreed.

"Another thing," I said. "Sam asked me if I would visit her sister in jail, which I did. As a result of that visit, I think I might be able to get some information on Star's neighbor, the one who may have molested Star."

"Better leave that to the police."

"The thing is, Sam and her sister are acquainted with a prostitute named Dolores who knows Star's neighbor. Dolores would never talk to the cops. So later tomorrow night, Sam's going with me to meet with Dolores. Then the two of them are going to see if they can find out more about Star's neighbor." I crossed my arms.

"Sounds like a terrible idea, but you've got that bullheaded look on your face." Jackie shook her head and scowled but didn't push it.

A short time later I parked Night Watch near the Ministry. I was on my own because Lydia had her get-together with her out-of-town friends. I saw Lawton sitting on the front steps, a couple of other gang members standing on the sidewalk next to him..

"Hey, guys," I said. "What's happening?"

"Can we talk private, Chaplain?" asked Lawton.

Five minutes later, we sat in a booth at Mo's drinking coffee.

"You doing okay?" I asked.

"Yeah. Johnson told me they're still lookin' at me, but I ain't so worried no more."

"Good. So what's on your mind?"

Lawton lit a cigarette. "I been thinkin' 'bout this neighbor of Star's. If I knew his name and what he looks like, I could try to find out what hooker he parties with. Maybe she'd help us find out if he did the murder. What do you think?"

The more I hung out with Lawton, the better I liked him. "I'm already working on it. I've talked to the woman he parties with and she's going to help."

"Cool. So what's the neighbor guy's name, and what does he look like?"

I hesitated. "Lawton, if I tell you, I have to know you wouldn't try anything stupid."

"I'm past that. I just wanna see the creep busted for what he did to Star. And if he killed Star and Cat, I wanna see him get sent up for that."

I told Lawton about Warren Van Boven, about Dolores, and the eavesdropping plan.

"Want me to watch your back?" asked Lawton.

I told him Dolores insisted that no one else be involved.

As I headed for River City after talking with Lawton, second thoughts kicked in. How reliable was he? Would he keep his mouth shut? Would he, despite what he'd said, do something stupid like going after Van Boven himself?

Stepping inside the lounge, I spotted the two high school classmates I frequently ran into here. They were in the middle of a theological debate regarding the doctrine of divine election. Ours was a denomination heavily influenced by John Calvin, a reformer who broke with the Catholic Church. My classmates often argued with each other as if competing for best-Calvinist award.

One of them was passionately making his point when we all paused to observe Sam approach the server station and set down her tray. She made motions of dancing and gave me a "come hither" look. I laughed, raised my beer glass to her and returned my attention to my classmate's argument.

He seemed to have forgotten the point he was making. "Hey, Reverend, you don't have a little something going on the side with the gorgeous Samantha, do you?"

"I wish." I was getting faster on my feet. I told them about dancing with Sam the previous week just before that *Times* reporter and I talked with them.

When Sam returned to the waitress station, I joined her. "I wanted to tell you that I'm coming in with my wife tomorrow night. I want Jackie to meet the woman who got me to dance for the first time, and I want you to meet Jackie."

Sam was not smiling, not flirting. "Okay," she said in a neutral tone. "I'd like to meet her."

"And, Sam, don't say anything about our plan with Dolores and Van Boven. I mentioned it to Jackie, but she'll worry too much if she knows the details."

CHAPTER 13

Sam and I are slow dancing. She's wearing a skimpy black dress. The bar is darker than usual. For some reason, we are alone in the bar. Sam slides her leg between my legs. We kiss deeply. I cup her butt with my right hand. With my left, I fondle her breast.

I feel a tapping on my shoulder and turn. It's Jackie. She says, "This must be the infamous Sam."

I awoke with a start, my heart racing. I lay there for a few minutes, breathing rapidly. Why did my unconscious bring Jackie into the dream? I hated it when I interrupted my sexy dreams that way. The price of being a good Calvinist?

My nose felt stuffy and my throat scratchy. I sneezed. Must have caught Andy's cold. As I showered, I realized I'd forgotten to tell Jackie that I'd sent the letter declining the call to Washington Avenue, and she'd already left for work.

In the kitchen I found a note from my mother-in-law. She and Andy were out for a walk. I downed a bowl of cereal and a cup of coffee, then left a note saying that I had gone to run some errands.

After lunch, with Andy down for his nap, my mother-in-law handed me the previous day's newspaper. On the front page was an article about the anti-war demonstration with a picture of Jackie and me holding hands. Behind us and slightly to the left, was the "Make Love Not War" poster. Jackie's mom said nothing.

"I've seen it," I said. I laid the paper on the coffee table and said goodbye. As I walked to my car, it hit me: *no call from my mother*. I must be in even more hot water with her than usual.

At the Ministry I met with a couple who wanted me to marry them in September. We talked about their relationship, about marriage and about the wedding plans.

After they left I got a call from my Urban Mission Committee chairman. He questioned my participation in the peace demonstration, but didn't seem terribly upset by it. I wondered if he was covering his butt.

Lawton showed up mid-afternoon. We got coffee and brought it to my office. He'd gotten his hair cut since I'd seen him the previous night. After a few minutes, he said, "I don't know where the hell to start."

"There's no wrong place to begin."

He sighed and settled into the chair, stretched out his long legs and crossed them at the ankles. "This is fuckin' hard. I'm not used to this. I'm not sure I can do it." He sat up straight, confusion in his eyes, then blurted, "I just want to change, clean up my act."

"I think you're changing already."

"You do? Oh, the haircut?"

"No. You seem different from when I first met you."

"I'm trying to get it together."

"It shows."

He shook his head like he couldn't quite believe it. "It's just that I don't know how I'm supposed to be. My old lady was a drunk. My old man was a rotten son of a bitch who beat her and knocked me around. I got into fights all the time when I was growin' up. Been busted twice for breaking and entering, twice for assault. I just figured, fuck people before they fuck you. Know what I mean?"

I nodded and kept my mouth shut. Lawton had never opened up like this, and I stayed out of his way.

"I joined a carnie crew when I was fourteen. Came to GR with a different carnival, got fired, joined the Night Stalkers. Gang members looked up to me. I knew how to handle myself. Guess it was all those years on the road. When Zeke got busted for second-degree murder and sent up to the joint, I got voted president. That's about the time I started runnin' into you guys from the Ministry. Thought you were all a bunch of flaming assholes—"

"Sometimes we are."

Lawton laughed. "Yeah, but I don't know. You guys just seem to accept us and even respect us. I never had that before. I thought Red Feather was as crazy as you Ministry guys, but I liked him, too. It's just that I don't know how I'm supposed to act no more. What am I supposed to do, Chaplain?"

I raised one eyebrow and flashed the peace sign.

Lawton erupted with a belly laugh. "Damn! Just when I got my hair cut! Can you see me with beads and a big peace sign on my shirt? Don't get me wrong. I like most of the heads. That's just not me."

He sobered again. "My old man told me never to piss upwind, but I think that's what I been doin'." He shook his head. "Jesus, this is hard. I guess I got a lot to think about. But even though it scares the shit out of me, it feels like I'm on the right track."

"Trust that feeling," I said, thinking how much I loved my job at times like this.

I pulled a tissue from the box on my desk and blew my nose. My cold was getting worse.

After warning me to be careful that night as I eavesdropped on Van Boven, Lawton left my office.

* * *

I was tense at supper. I worried about Jackie's reaction to Sam and about Sam's reaction to Jackie. I worried about the plan to catch Van Boven incriminating himself.

Just as Andy's sitter arrived, the phone rang. "I stopped at the Corner Pocket on the way home from work," said Lydia. "Ronnie was there. I asked Ronnie about the guy who badmouthed the downtown kids and the Ministry. He said the guy was maybe in his forties, red hair, balding and his face looks like he'd had a bad case of adolescent acne."

"That's a perfect description of Star's neighbor, the guy I told you about."

"Good luck tonight. If this guy did kill the girls, I hope you get the goods on him. See you tomorrow night."

Driving to River City Lounge a few minutes later, I kept glancing at Jackie. She looked gorgeous, dressed in a denim skirt that came just above her knees and a light blue sleeveless top. She wore small gold earrings and had her hair in a long braid. We entered the bar and found a table near the dance floor.

Jackie took my hand. "I can't believe I finally get to dance with you."

Sam approached our table. "Hi, Rob. This must be Jackie." They shook hands. Sam laughed. "I don't know how you dare let this good-looking guy hang out at night in the places he does. You really ought to keep a tighter leash on him."

Jackie smiled. "Yes, if he's running into attractive women like you, maybe you're right."

"Seriously, you're lucky to have each other."

"I think so, too," said Jackie. "So, you got this guy out on the dance floor, huh?"

"Had to sneak up on him, but he did pretty good for an uptight Dutchman. You guys want something to drink?"

To the sound of "Love Potion Number Nine," I took Jackie's hand, and we stepped over to the dance floor. We stayed there for the Beatles' "All You Need Is Love" and then returned to our table.

"This is fun," I said. "Let's do it for a whole evening soon. Maybe Blaine and his wife can join us."

Sam came to check on us. "You guys are looking good out there," she said. "Can I get you anything else?"

"No," said Jackie. "We have to run. But thanks for getting this guy off his duff."

"I'll be back to pick you up in a little while," I said to Sam.

* * *

I drove with Sam to Memorial Park and left the car there. It was a balmy night, and Sam wore an outfit as skimpy as her work uniform. While we walked down South Division to the Alibi, I thought about Ronnie shooting pool with Van Boven. At least I was ninety-nine percent certain it was Van Boven he'd described to Lydia. If Van Boven wanted gang kids, hippies and the Street Ministry eliminated, maybe he had taken matters into his own hands. And if he had a thing for young girls … I shuddered to think who might be next.

We turned a block before the Alibi and walked up the alley to the parking lot behind the bar. There were four cars in the small lot and another half dozen spaces open. Sam went inside to see if Dolores was there while I scouted the area behind the trash bins. The containers stood a foot to a foot and a half from the back wall of the building. I eased myself into the opening, trying to avoid stepping on trash that littered the ground. A scurrying sound put my heart in my throat. The stench made my stomach churn. A faint sound of music from the bar drifted on the night air.

The back door of the bar opened and closed, the music getting louder, then quieter. A whisper, "Think the Reverend fell into the garbage?"

Sam and Dolores giggled. I poked my head out and saw them looking at me. I was about to wave when headlights turned into the alley. I ducked my head back.

A car door slammed, and a guy who didn't sound anything like Van Boven said, "Looks like my timing is perfect. You two babes want to party?"

"Fuck off, honky. We're havin' a private talk here," said Dolores.

"Maybe later," he said. The door of the bar opened and closed.

I heard Dolores say, "Just follow my lead, Sam—I mean Sandra—and you'll do fine."

That sounded like a good idea to me, not using Sam's real name.

Time dragged until another set of headlights turned into the alley. Sam and Dolores continued to talk, laughing like two girlfriends, as another customer exited his car and entered the bar. I was about to poke my head out again when a third vehicle pulled in. This time, when a car door opened and closed, a man's voice said, "Hey, Dolores."

"How they hangin', Charlie? This is Sandra. We bumped into each other and was catchin' up. I told her I was expectin' somebody, and maybe he'd be interested in a little three-way party. What you think, Charlie?"

I imagined Van Boven giving Sam the once-over.

"Maybe," he said. "I've had some great fantasies about having a party with you and a younger girl."

Sam laughed. "I guess I'm too old for him, Dolores."

"I'm not saying that. I just like a little teenage pussy once in a while."

Dolores snorted. "Yeah, like you ever had any teenage pussy!"

"I've been getting it on with my neighbor girl. She can't get enough of me."

I imagined Van Boven puffing out his chest.

"Yeah? How old was she when you started doin' her?"

"Fourteen, fifteen."

"Charlie, Charlie," Dolores said in a mocking tone. "If this neighbor girl can't get enough of you, go get her and we'll party."

"Afraid I can't do that. She's one of those kids that got murdered downtown. We'll have to find some other young girl."

"She threaten to rat on you? You take care of that little problem?" Dolores's tone had changed to one of respect. "Maybe you more a man than I thought."

"No! I didn't kill her. The bitch threatened to turn me in though, so somebody did me a favor. I'm getting a hard-on just talking with you two. Maybe a change of pace would be nice. How about it Sandra? You got a place the two of us can party?"

I felt the sneeze coming. I pinched my nose and stifled all but a tiny sound.

Sam squealed, "Look, it's a rat."

"Forget that rat, Sandra," said Dolores. "This honky rat wants to party with you. Guess I know when I ain't wanted."

The door to the bar opened and closed.

"How about it, Sandra?"

"I don't steal johns from friends, Charlie." Once again the back door of the bar opened and closed.

I wondered if Van Boven would follow the women into the bar, but I heard him mutter something, get back into his car and drive out of the lot. Sliding out from behind the trash containers, I entered the bar and sat down with Sam and Dolores.

Sam laughed. "I told him I don't steal johns from friends."

Dolores hooted.

"How did you like the way Dolores worked him, Rob. Isn't she amazing?"

Dolores snorted. "It's true, I'm amazing. But I told you, Rob, how he's always braggin' 'bout stuff. That's why it was so easy. What the hell was that sound you made?"

"I sneezed," I said, mopping my nose with my hanky.

Dolores shook her head. "At least he copped to fuckin' the girl."

"Doesn't sound like he murdered Star, though," said Sam.

Dolores stretched and yawned. "Yeah, that's a bummer, 'cause I know that's what you were really after. You need some cheering up? You guys want to go to my crib for a little fun?"

"Thanks, Dolores," I said. "I think you're a very sexy woman, but I'd better get going."

Sam grinned at me, but spoke to Dolores. "Rob's got it bad for me, Dolores. He might not want to share me."

I don't blush easily, but I felt the heat rise from my neck to my face.

Sam and I walked back to my car. She was high on our little escapade and chattered about what a great detective team the three of us had been.

I didn't share her enthusiasm. "Van Boven could deny the whole thing. He could claim he didn't know how old Star was, say he was just blowing smoke. I'll tell Johnson about it, but I doubt anything would hold up in court. And I'm no closer to knowing who murdered the girls."

In the lot by the rear entrance to River City, Sam hopped out. She leaned down, to look in the open passenger window, increasing her already ample cleavage. "You brought Jackie to the bar to try to cool things between us. Did it work?"

I hesitated, forcing myself not to stare at her breasts.

"That's what I thought," she said and walked to the back door of the bar, turned to wave, and went inside.

I didn't want to think about what Sam had just asked me. Instead, I reviewed what I'd heard Van Boven say about Star. Despite his denial, I still wondered if he might have killed her.

Suddenly, the passenger door of my car opened. Van Boven slid in, pointing a gun at me.

CHAPTER 14

"Start the car, Reverend," said Van Boven. "I'll tell you where to drive."

I followed his directions through downtown. We were soon on the River Road, river on one side, woods on the other, five lonely miles between Grand Rapids and Grandville.

"Thought you'd get me to admit murdering the Wynsma girl, did you? I got suspicious when I left the lot at the Alibi. Waited on the street till I saw you and Sandra come out, and I followed you. You were the *rat* behind the trash."

I caught a glimpse of the Grand River through the trees. Would my body be found floating in the river?

"Okay," I said, "you figured it out. Since you didn't murder anyone, you've got nothing to worry about. So why are we taking this ride and why the gun?"

"Don't play dumb with me, Vander Laan. You heard me admit to having sex with the Wynsma girl. I can't just let that go."

"But she's dead. That's water under the bridge. I'm only concerned about the murder." Not exactly the truth.

"I can't take that chance. I'm not worried about the testimony of two whores, but you're a different story. Now slow down."

We were in the Indian mounds area, where two low hills were evidence of early Indian culture. I was pretty sure this was also the area with the gravel pit where the Lost Souls came to swim and drink. I glimpsed a distant light in my mirror and prayed for rescue.

"Just a little further. There it is. Turn left and follow that two-track."

I touched the brake several times, hoping whoever was behind me would catch my signal.

Talk about wishful thinking. What would I do if I were behind a car that turned into the woods here at this time of night? Keep on going, that's what I'd do.

As I drove slowly over the two-track, the trees thinned out into a clearing. I saw moonlight on water. Probably the Souls' swimming hole. I prayed they'd come for a swim now.

"Shut the lights off and kill the engine," said Van Boven. "Put the keys in your pocket. Now sit there and don't move."

He got out, came around to my side, and motioned with the gun for me to get out. He stepped back just as the thought of smashing the door into him crossed my mind.

When I got out of the car he said, "Now back up slowly toward the water."

He was sweating and the hand pointing the gun at me was shaking. I heard the sounds of crickets and frogs and my heart thudding in my chest. The moon passed behind a cloud.

"Hiding behind the garbage bin was smart, I have to admit," he said.

This is where I should keep him talking. At least that's how it went in the movies. My tongue was tied in a knot, my mouth dry. It was like a bad dream, but I was ready to wake up, forget the whole detective thing, stick to my job of ministry.

Pray, that's what I should do. *Help*!

I heard a twig snap. Van Boven looked around cautiously, keeping the gun pointed at me. We listened to the croak of bullfrogs and a sniffling sound—possibly a raccoon or possum.

Van Boven turned his full attention back to me. "This is the way it's going to play. You came out here for a swim, but you had a little accident. Hit your head on a rock when you dived in, and you drowned. You really shouldn't have come out here by yourself at night. Just your unorthodox nature, I guess. But a shame, all the same."

He leaned down and picked up a rock the size of his fist. "Now take off your clothes. Lay them over that log there," he said pointing to his left with the gun.

I took a few steps toward the log. *Think of something*, I screamed silently. I pulled my shirt over my head and dropped it. I sat down on the log, ready to untie my shoes.

"You have a chance to make this right, Van Boven, or at least make up some for what you did to Susan." The words came in a rush. "You can come clean to the police. You can ask Susan's parents to forgive you. You can ask God to forgive you. I'll help you get through this."

Van Boven snorted. He was shaking more and had a wild look in his eyes. "You're out of your gourd. I'm not going to let my name be smeared by this. I've just been elected to be a deacon at my church. Even if charges for statutory rape didn't stick, you could screw things up for me in all kinds of ways. It's going to happen like I said. A fatal accident."

"If you kill me, you might as well kiss your life goodbye. You'll never get away with it. The police already suspect you of murdering both girls. When my body is found, they'll never believe it was an accident." Would he buy the bluff?

"We've wasted enough time. Take your pants off and do it now." He waved the gun at me.

I realized I had nothing to lose. I was going to die. But Van Boven did not want to shoot me. He wanted it to look like an accident.

"No," I said and stood up. "I don't think I want to take that swim. You'll just have to shoot me." I felt giddy.

Van Boven was surprisingly fast as he stepped forward, his hand with the rock flying toward my head.

Suddenly, a yell, "Drop it, Van Boven!"

He whirled. I heard gunshots as I dodged to my right, tripped and went down, hitting my forehead on something hard.

My head hurt like blazes. I felt blood dripping down my face. The moon passed from behind the clouds as I got to my hands and knees and then carefully stood up, swaying. Van Boven lay sprawled on his back over the log I'd been sitting on a moment before, blood dripping from his temple, over his ear. His gun rested a few feet from his hand. I reached down and felt a pulse. He was breathing shallowly. I grabbed the shirt I'd taken off a moment before and used it to pick up the gun, not wanting my fingerprints on it. Looking toward my car, I saw someone struggling to get to his feet.

As I walked unsteadily toward him he staggered to my car, leaned against it for support, and looked at me. "You okay, Chaplain?"

"I think so, Lawton. Great timing." I wiped blood from my eyes with my hand. "You okay?"

"Bastard got me in the leg. Is he dead?"

"No. He's breathing."

I opened my car door and placed Van Boven's gun under the driver's seat, pushing back the other weapons I'd collected and forgotten about.

"I'd better get you guys to the ER," I said. I dragged Van Boven to my car, then leaned against it, dizzy and panting, as Lawton limped over. Together, we managed to get Van Boven into the back seat. Lawton eased into the front seat, dragging his wounded leg in after him. I had a hard time see-ing because of the blood dripping into my eyes. I folded my shirt into a strip and tied it around my head.

"What about your gun," I asked as I started the car.

"I'll hang on to it in case the bastard comes around."

"Grab that rag under your seat and wrap it around your leg," I said.

Driving back into town, I wanted to ask Lawton how he happened to show up at the gravel pit, but when I glanced at him, his eyes were closed and I decided to wait.

When we reached the ER, Van Boven was still uncon-scious. Lawton was pale and shaking. I asked him to slide his gun under the seat and then walked into the hospital and reported to the nurse at the desk. She led me to an examining room as other ER personnel rushed out to bring in the two injured men.

* * *

"Like to ask him a few questions, Doc," said the cop. "Okay with you?"

The intern had finished stitching my forehead, and a uni-formed officer stood at the foot of the stretcher I was lying on.

"As soon as I'm finished, he's all yours," said the intern. Then, to me, "I'm going to keep you here until we get the x-rays back. If there's no problem, you can be on your way."

I reached out a hand to delay him. "Do you know how Lawton and Van Boven are, the two guys I brought in with gunshot wounds?"

"Mr. Lawton was lucky that the bullet went through his calf and didn't hit any major arteries. We'll want to keep him overnight because his blood pressure's low, but he'll probably be discharged tomorrow, barring complications.

"The other bullet tore Mr. Van Boven's scalp pretty good and left a bunch of bone splinters to dig out of the wound. Picking all those splinters out of blood and hair was a bit of a hassle. He's lucky the bullet didn't go through his skull. Now he's having a hard time breathing, and I can't figure out why. Did he fall on anything that might have injured some ribs?"

"A log."

"That could explain it." He smiled a tired smile and left the cubicle.

I told the officer the whole story and that the guns were under the front seat of my car. I answered his questions and suggested he inform Detective Johnson. The officer took some notes, wrote down my name, address, phone numbers, and left.

A nurse came in. "Rob, you doing okay?" It was Brandon Sharpe's wife.

"I'm fine. I didn't know you worked here."

She moved close to get a better look at the stitches, then got some gauze and tape from a drawer and covered the wound, then wrapped a strip of gauze around my head. She gave me her appraising look but said nothing further.

As she started to leave, I said, "Think I could see Lawton?"

"He's being admitted. You'll have to wait until morning."

A moment after she stepped out, Stu Peterson came in. "Caught it on the police scanner, Rob. You feeling well enough to tell me what happened?"

I told the story again.

After Stu left, the intern came back and told me my x-rays were negative but to return if I experienced nausea or dizziness. He also told me to have my doctor take out the stitches in a week or ten days. As the intern left, the uniformed officer came back and reported he'd talked to Johnson who wanted to see me at the station in the morning.

When I got home, I put my bloody shirt in the kitchen sink to soak. I took a beer from a fresh six-pack in the refrigerator and sat at the table, not bothering to turn the light on. I felt exhausted and depressed. What had I accomplished as far as the murders were concerned?

I made my decision as I finished my third beer. I'd risked too much already. No more amateur detective stuff. Leave it to the police.

I was sitting in the dark, finishing the last of the six-pack and feeling no pain when Jackie came down the stairs and into the kitchen. She switched the light on. I closed my eyes against the sudden illumination, blinking them open gradually. Jackie turned pale and her mouth gaped. She glanced at the sink with my shirt soaking in the bloody water, then looked at the bandage wrapped around my head. She dropped into a chair next to me and took my hand. "Oh, honey, what happened to you?"

So I told the story again, but less coherently than at the hospital. Somewhere during my narrative, Jackie dropped my hand and moved back in her chair. When I finished, she studied me, then looked at the empty beer cans on the table, emotions surfing rapidly across her face—confusion, fear, love, anger.

The anger settled. "How could you be so stupid!" Her voice was barely above a whisper, but it was worse than if she'd screamed at me. "Taking a chance like that! Didn't you think about me, about your son? Why couldn't you leave it to the police? And this!" Her hand swept over the empty beer cans.

"I felt like I had to do something, Jacks. Like I owed it to Star and Cat." It sounded lame to me, and I could see it did to Jackie, too.

She shook her head and scrubbed her face with her hands. "Maybe your mother and my mom are right. Maybe you should take the call to Washington Avenue."

I winced.

"You decided to decline the call, and you sent the letter."

I nodded.

"And just when were you going to tell me?"

"Tomorrow." I looked at my watch. "Today, actually."

"Maybe you need to think about the Jamestown church. If they'd even have you now! If any church would! Maybe we should just … I don't know. I can't talk about it any more tonight. Let's go to bed."

After laboring up the stairs behind Jackie, I undressed and fell into an exhausted sleep.

* * *

I woke with a nasty headache. I groaned. Andy ran into the bedroom, stopping suddenly. A look of alarm came over his face. "Daddy, you got an owie."

I sat on the edge of the bed, and Andy climbed onto my lap. "I bet a big hug from you will help it feel better."

Andy hugged me tightly. "How did you get your owie, Daddy?"

Looking up, I saw Jackie standing in the doorway. "Daddy fell and hit his head on a rock," she said.

"Shall I kiss it, Daddy?"

"I'd like that." Andy kissed the bandage very gently. "It feels better already. Thank you, Andy."

I took a couple aspirin, then went down to the kitchen. Jackie and I sat at the table drinking coffee while Andy watched cartoons in the living room.

"Sorry I was so hard on you last night," she said. "I was just so darn scared and so mad at you for taking such dumb risks and then getting drunk. You have to promise me you won't play detective anymore."

"Do you understand why I felt I had to do what I could to stop the murders and find out who did it?"

"I guess some sense of owing it to the kids you work with."

"Yes, it's partly that. But even more, I owed it to myself. I couldn't live with myself if I hadn't done something."

"But weren't you scared? I mean, hiding behind the trash bin with a possible murderer a few feet away from you?"

"That part wasn't so bad, but the gravel pit …"

Jackie looked at me intently. "So it sounds like it was, I don't know, a matter of personal integrity for you."

"Yes." It was clearer to me now, too. I rubbed my fingers lightly over the bandage, trying to soothe the headache. "Just give me a little more time to sort things out before I promise anything."

"Your integrity is one of the reasons I married you. Now I'm not sure I can live with the stupid risks you're taking because of your stupid integrity."

"What do you mean, not sure you can live with it?" My gut suddenly felt hollow.

"I don't know. I want to support you, but I need some time with this."

I put aside my dread regarding our next discussion. "I want to run over to the hospital now and see Lawton."

"Tell him I said thanks for saving your stupid life."

Before I left, I called John Vanden Berg, Van Boven's pastor, and filled him in. "I wanted you to know," I said, "in case you want to make a hospital call on your parishioner."

John was silent for a moment, probably stunned. Then he thanked me for calling him.

When I hung up, I remembered my parents. Better call them before they heard on the news or via the Dutch grapevine about my almost being killed by Van Boven.

I should have known. One of the nurses who worked in the ER was related to someone in Dad's congregation, and I was too late. I had to listen to Mother's chastisement for not calling sooner and for further hurting my reputation in the denomination.

I was prepared for Mother to upbraid me for my lack of patriotism as shown by my participation in the anti-war protest. Not a word. I was certain she knew about my involvement because the grapevine wouldn't miss such a tidbit. Since mother got on my case at every opportunity, perhaps her silence about the demonstration answered a question my classmates and I had debated at seminary: Exactly what is the "unpardonable sin?"

CHAPTER 15

"Hey, Chaplain. How's the head?" At the hospital I'd found Lawton in his room, dressed and sitting in a chair. Crutches leaned against the wall next to him.

I smiled. "Okay. How's the leg?"

"They tell me I'll live. I'm leavin' as soon as they bring a wheelchair."

"Can you walk?"

"Just got a hell of a limp. They want me to use crutches for a while."

"How are you getting to your place?"

"Nurse is callin' a cab."

"Want me to drop you instead?"

"Johnson called and wants me to go see him as soon as they let me out of this place."

"I've got to see him, too. We can go together. How come you showed up at the gravel pit last night?"

"I know you told me to stay out of it, but I still figured you could use some back-up. I followed you and the hot babe to the Alibi. When you went to drop her off at River City, I followed you on my bike. I stayed out of sight because I didn't want you to get pissed at me. I was ready to split when I saw Van Boven get in the car with you, so I followed you guys to the gravel pit. You know the rest."

"Is that gravel pit the Souls' party spot?"

"One of 'em."

Lawton had the nurse cancel the taxi and we left the hospital. On the way to the police station, I learned that Lawton, too, had been eavesdropping on Van Boven from where he'd squirreled himself between the Alibi and the building next door. That made four potential witnesses on a molestation charge, but I doubted it would ever come to trial with the victim dead and nothing but hearsay evidence.

I waited in the lobby while Lawton was interviewed. I glanced with little interest through the sports section of a newspaper that someone had left. Denny McClain had chalked up another win for the Tigers. I wondered if he'd do the impossible and beat his record of the previous season when the Tigers had also won the Series. I looked up and saw Lawton swing toward me on his crutches.

"How'd it go?" I asked.

"Pretty good. I don't think Johnson's gonna lean on me too much about the gun. Of course they'll have to hang on to it for evidence. I ain't happy about that. Johnson don't seem to have such a hard on for me no more though."

Kincaid appeared, signaled me, and I followed him along the familiar route to the Detective Bureau. Johnson waved me toward a chair. Kincaid sat down at the desk next to Johnson's, grabbed a pen and notebook, and swung his chair in our direction. Meanwhile, Johnson shuffled through some papers for a few minutes. Then he drilled me about the previous night for what seemed like a long while, repeating some questions several times.

Finally, he leaned forward, elbows on the desk. "So could you see Van Boven from where you were hiding?"

"No."

"Did you recognize his voice?" asked Kincaid.

"I guess I couldn't swear to that. I only heard him speak that one time at Star's funeral, and he barely said anything."

Johnson flipped through the papers he'd been shuffling. "Now, about the arsenal under the seat of your car. Yeah, here it is. Two guns, three knives and a chain. Outlaw identified his gun, so the thirty-two automatic must be Van Boven's. These other weapons yours?"

"Um, not exactly."

Johnson rolled his eyes and sighed.

I glanced at Kincaid who shook his head, looking bemused.

First I described Arnold's knife. Johnson already knew that story. "I took the other knives and the chain from, ah, a couple of guys who were about to get into it with each other. I didn't plan to leave the weapons in my car. I forgot about them."

Johnson scowled. "Who were the guys who were about to get into it with each other?"

I crossed my arms.

Johnson stared at me. I'd been skewered with the stare by better than him. My mother used to drill me with the silent stare to get me to talk when I'd done something I didn't want to own up to. It worked till I was nine.

"Look, Detective, " I finally said, "if I answered your question, I couldn't do my job. And that would mean more trouble for the police."

Johnson was silent for another moment, then apparently decided to drop the matter. He shifted in his chair. "How would you like to go with us this afternoon to the Wynsma's to tell them about their perverted neighbor?"

I shot him a look of surprise. "Yes, I'll do that."

"We'll pick you up at your house."

When my interview was finished, Lawton and I left the station. He directed me to the new pad the Souls had moved to. I parked in front. "Thanks for saving my butt, man," I said. "Seems like there's been so much happening I haven't even gotten around to thanking you till now. Jackie says to tell you thanks, too."

He looked tired. "We did good, huh?"

When I walked into my house a short time later, the phone was ringing. Brandon Sharp offered his support and pressed me for every detail of my encounter with Van Boven. Something about that made me uneasy, but I figured it was just his way of showing interest.

"I have some friends in law enforcement," he said, "and I've done a lot of reading on the subject. I have to tell you that, from everything you said, Van Boven's got to be your killer, despite his denial. I suspect Star was his first victim and he got a taste for it. So his motive for killing that second girl was to relive the thrill. I wouldn't be surprised if that was part of the motive for his attempt to kill you, too."

I hadn't thought of that. "Maybe you're right."

"I think you know me well enough to recognize that I only have your best interests at heart when I say, leave the detective work to the cops. That isn't your job. You were lucky you came out of it as well as you did. You have a family to think about. Plus, that kind of risky behavior on your part could jeopardize our church support and your future as a Christian Reformed minister."

"I'll keep your advice in mind."

At lunch I had the feeling that Jackie was keeping up a front of normalcy for Andy's sake. As I put Andy down for his nap, he made his usual solemn pronouncement: "I'm not sleeping, Daddy. I'm just going to rest." When I came back down to the living room, Jackie was sitting on the couch doing nothing.

Jackie almost never did nothing. I figured she must be very upset.

Grabbing a tissue from the box on the end table and blowing my nose, I sat down on the couch beside her. Neither of us spoke for a moment. A single tear ran down her cheek and she swiped a hand at it. "I was so scared. I could have lost you."

She began to cry harder and I reached out to hold her. She stopped me with a raised hand. After a few minutes, she took a deep breath and regained her composure.

"I can sort of see why you had to do what you did," she said, looking into my eyes. "That doesn't mean I like it. What Lydia said about your connections with people and getting information makes sense, too. Just be careful, will you?"

"That's a promise I can make."

Later I was in the study upstairs, perusing the last few issues of *The Banner*, our denominational periodical, when the front doorbell rang. I headed downstairs and found Johnson and Kincaid introducing themselves to Jackie.

* * *

Johnson drove in silence for a while. I sat in the back seat, wondering if I should try to make conversation. After a while Johnson heaved a sigh. "I have to tell you, Reverend Vander Laan, these two homicides are getting to me."

"Because you haven't solved the case yet?" I said.

"Yeah, but there's more to it than that."

"What do you mean?"

"To be honest, at first I didn't care that much. It's not like the brass is leaning on us a lot to clear this thing up. I mean, a couple less gang kids, what's the big deal? Don't get me wrong. Kincaid and I were still doing our jobs, but fewer gang kids means less trouble for us cops. Anyways, I guess I never really knew any of these kids before. Never knew you guys at the Street Ministry either."

"Are you saying that knowing people personally instead of by reputation makes a difference in how you feel about a case?"

Johnson grunted. I took that as a "yes."

"You and your colleagues don't have the most stellar reputation at the Department," put in Kincaid.

"We're probably seen as liberal pussies who coddle a bunch of useless scum," I said.

Kincaid whipped around to look at me.

"You been listening to the locker room conversation?" laughed Johnson. "I've heard it put exactly that way." After a moment of silence, he said, "I didn't know the Wynsma girl or Cat, but I gotta tell you, this Red Feather, he seems to have his head screwed on pretty good. I thought Lawton was a dirt bag. Now, I don't know what to make of him."

"Lawton is going through the changes," I said. "It's no wonder you don't know what to make of him. He's trying to clean up his act."

"Anyways," said Johnson, "I just don't want to see another one of these kids get whacked."

"I don't know where you are with Van Boven as a suspect," I said. "One of my board members thinks Van Boven murdered both girls, and that, in killing Star, he discovered the thrill of killing."

Johnson just grunted and Kincaid said nothing, so I hadn't the foggiest what they thought of Brandon's ideas.

At the Wynsma house, Johnson rang the bell. Corey appeared and ushered us in.

Alice greeted the detectives, then turned to me. "Detective Kincaid told us you were coming with them. What happened?" She pointed to the bandage on my forehead, and suddenly I noticed how tight the stitches felt.

"I'll tell you in a minute, Alice."

Corey indicated we should sit, moved to the couch with Alice, and took her hand. "Have you caught our daughter's killer, Detective Johnson?" he asked.

"No, but we're doing everything we can. We came to talk to you about another matter related to Susan. I asked Reverend Vander Laan to come along and tell you about it."

Corey and Alice turned to me expectantly.

I cleared my throat. "I'm not sure how to say this. I'm afraid it's more bad news. It concerns Susan and your neighbor, Warren Van Boven."

Alice gripped her husband's hand more tightly. "How can it be bad news regarding the two of them? I don't understand."

"Warren was sexually molesting Susan," I said.

Alice turned pale and her body stiffened "No. It can't be."

Corey's face and neck turned red. "That son-of-a-bitch!" He spat out the words. Turning to Alice he said, "It could explain some things, like Susan suddenly starting to hang out downtown." He turned back to me. "It was to get away from him, wasn't it?"

"No! She would have told us!" insisted Alice.

"Is Susan's sister around right now?" I asked.

"Judy's with her aunt in Cadillac." Alice's eyes grew wide with alarm. "Why?"

"Warren threatened to hurt Judy. That's why Susan didn't tell."

Alice held a hand over her mouth and seemed to take no notice of the tears that spilled down her cheeks as she comprehended the horror. She looked at Corey, whose face was still red.

"That son-of-a-bitch," he said again, more quietly this time. "Have you arrested him, Detective?"

"He's in the hospital," said Johnson, "recovering from a gunshot wound. When he's released, he'll probably be charged with attempted murder. I'm afraid that with Susan dead, we won't be able to charge him with statutory rape. The prosecutor will have to decide about the charges."

"Gunshot wound? Attempted murder?" Alice looked from Johnson to me.

"Guess you'd better tell the whole story, Reverend Vander Laan," said Johnson.

"Sounds like you haven't caught the news yet today," I said.

Corey and Alice shook their heads.

I gave an abbreviated version of what had happened the night before, then looked at Johnson, handing the ball back to him.

"As I said, when Mr. Van Boven gets out of the hospital, we'll probably book him for attempted murder. And despite his denials, we haven't ruled him out as Susan's killer. He may have had motive if Susan threatened to expose him."

"I know it's not Christian," said Corey, "but I hope they lock him up and throw away the key. He made out like he was a big confidant for our daughter." He shook his head, a look of disgust on his face.

"This guy who saved your life," Alice said to me, "is he the president of the Lost Souls, one of the kids who was at the funeral?"

"Yes. Lawton. His nickname used to be Outlaw."

"And a prostitute and a cocktail waitress helped you get Warren to admit that he and Susan were …?" Alice looked incredulous.

"Yes."

Alice shook her head. "We should have seen what was happening with Susan. We should have done something." She buried her head in her hands and sobbed.

When Kincaid started to say something I put my hand up to silence him, and we waited till Alice's crying subsided.

I spoke quietly. "Alice, look at me, please." She slowly raised her eyes to me. "If you're a loving parent, you're going to feel guilty." I glanced at Corey to include him. "I can't erase your guilt, but you have to realize that there is nothing you could have done. You couldn't know. Over time, you'll have to work at forgiving yourself."

Alice said nothing.

The two detectives spent the next several minutes questioning Cory and Alice about Van Boven and Susan. Finally, Johnson stood. Kincaid and I followed suit. "Anyways," said Johnson, "you'll be contacted about the charges against Mr. Van Boven. If you think of anything else about him and Susan, get a hold of me or Detective Kincaid."

As we stepped out the door, I picked up the *Times* from the top step and handed it to Corey. A picture of me in my clerical shirt, taken a few months earlier, was on the front page. The headline read: STREET MINISTER SAVED BY LOST SOUL. Cute. It had Stu Peterson's by-line.

As Johnson drove back to my house, he said, "You did okay with the Wynsmas, Reverend Vander Laan. You know, you might as well call me Sid." He tossed Kincaid a look I couldn't read. "That's what all the *other* detectives call me."

I laughed. "Then I guess you guys better call me Rob. Pretty much everybody calls me that."

Kincaid turned in his seat. I thought he was going to give me his first name, but he didn't. After a second he turned around again.

"One other thing then, Rob," said Johnson gruffly. "It might be better if next time you get these detective urges, you give me a jingle. After all, when I figured some ministering needed doing, I called you."

I laughed again. "Thanks for the advice, Sid." I was making no promises.

When he pulled up in front of my house, Johnson said, "You know …" He was silent for a moment. "I kinda get what the Wynsmas are going through. I lost my son a few years ago. You probably know about that." He studied the dashboard.

Kincaid looked out his window as if my house held great interest for him.

I wanted to give the big detective a hug, but I hardly dared say anything. It felt like a delicate moment when he could easily pull even deeper into his shell.

Finally I just said, "I do know and I'm sorry."

Jackie was dusting in the living room when I walked in. "How did it go with the Wynsmas?" she asked.

"They were pretty devastated, as you can imagine."

"How did it go with the detectives? I know you and Detective Johnson haven't been great fans of each other. I thought he seemed okay."

"Oh, Sid was fine. We got along good."

"Sid, huh? That sounds like an improvement. Oh, Lydia called. She read the story in the paper about you and wondered how you're doing. I invited her to come for dinner tomorrow. I told her you'd call her if you weren't feeling well enough for night ministry tonight."

"My cold is already doing better, and my forehead isn't bothering me at all. With my head bandage, maybe people who want to start a conversation will ask about that instead of focusing on my collar." I leaned in to give Jackie a hug, but she stopped me with her hands lightly pressed to my shoulders. "Want to talk more?" I asked "About us, I mean."

"Not yet."

How much trouble was our marriage in?

CHAPTER 16

"That's going to leave a heck of a scar," said Jackie as she changed the dressing on my head while I sat at the kitchen table. "I'm going to get real tired of your jokes about the bar fight and the "other guy" when people ask you about it. The wound looks good, though. Come to my office on Friday to have the stitches taken out."

After a brief visit from Blaine and his wife and three calls from concerned board members, I was on my way out the door when Jackie called me back in. My Urban Mission Committee chair was on the phone. He asked how I was doing after the attempt on my life and extended his support. Then he said, "I've gotten two angry calls from John since we talked last. I told him I was going to tell you. He was furious about your participation in the anti-war protest. He said that was *not* ministry, and you put a black mark on the denomination's reputation by being so unpatriotic. I told him I'd already talked with you about it. Then he called today after your almost getting killed last night by one of his church members. Again, his complaint was that you are not doing ministry, and he said the churches could not continue to pay you for such travesty."

"What did you tell him?"

"I promised we'd discuss these things more thoroughly at our next meeting. You'd better plan for at least an hour at the September session."

I reported the conversation to Jackie. "You'd think the son-of-a-bitch would talk to me instead of going behind my back."

"Come on," she said. "My memory of John from high school is that he was never straightforward and direct. Regardless, you could be jeopardizing your job by playing detective. John has some powerful connections. And, knowing John, he's not afraid to use them."

I felt that hard knot in my stomach again. John wasn't going to detract me from doing whatever I could to stop the murders of my congregation and finding out who the killer was.

Finally I left the house. At Drop-in, my first night ministry stop with Lydia, a large group of kids surrounded Lawton. I watched for a moment from the doorway. Lawton's feigned nonchalance could not mask his pleasure at all the attention he was getting. When I came into the room, a cheer went up. People hugged me, shook my hand, patted my back, asked me to tell what had happened. It was a bit overwhelming, but it warmed my heart.

Later, Stu Peterson and a *Times* photographer arrived. They took several pictures of Lawton in his colors and me in mine.

Finally Lydia and I were able to get away. River City Lounge was packed. Melvina Reynolds, singing "Little Boxes" came over the sound system. We made our way toward the bar and waved at the bartender over the heads of customers already lined up there. He said something to the two guys sitting in front of us. They picked up their glasses, raised a cheerful toast toward us, and vacated their stools. The bartender said he'd heard of my "adventure" on the news. He drew a couple of drafts for us as Sam approached.

Lydia and I shouted a greeting over the noise.

Sam looked at me with concern. "I couldn't believe it when I read the story in the paper today. I was so … I mean, seriously …" She threw her arms around me, then turned to greet Lydia. "Oh, my order's up. Let me know if you need anymore help with detecting." She went off with a tray full of drinks.

I talked with the two guys who'd given up their seats, supporting one of them as he shared his fears for his brother fighting in Viet Nam. Meanwhile, Lydia moved down the bar to the server station. I noticed her chatting with Sam whenever she came there with empties or to pick up an order. When we returned to my car, I told Lydia about taking Jackie to River City to meet Sam.

"So did it cool things between you and Sam?"

"I think so." I wondered if it had. Changing the subject, I said, "You and Sam really seem to be hitting it off."

"Yes, we are. She'd like to help us catch the murderer. I think she likes to take risks, and she'd practically do anything for you."

I shot Lydia a skeptical look.

"Oh, yes," she said. "Sam told me about you helping her with that drug overdose when the attorney she was seeing dumped her. She said you waited for hours with her at the emergency room and helped her talk it all through afterwards. She also told me about you bringing her to talk to Nathan when she was on that bad acid trip. I don't think you should take her flirting too seriously, though. I watched her tonight, and she's that way with most guys."

"You're probably right." I fired up the engine. "I'd like to try to touch bases with Dolores if we can."

At the Alibi we nursed our beers at the bar for a while and talked with a guy sporting a big Afro. No sign of Dolores. Two beers was my limit, well, aside from the previous night in my kitchen, so I suggested to Lydia that we move on.

We hit a few more bars, talked with several people, and one guy bent our ears for half an hour with a drunken story of his bad marriage.

As I drove up Division Avenue toward town, I spotted Dolores on the corner by Amigos Bar. I pulled to the curb, and she rapidly walked away. She must not have noticed the less than subtle ways my car differed from Vice Squad cars. I drove slowly, keeping up with her. "Dolores," I yelled, "it's just me."

She came over to the car when I pulled into a no-parking zone. She squatted down next to the passenger door. "Oh, honey. I'm sure glad you're okay. I nearly died when I heard on the news about what happened to you after you left last night. You sure you're all right?"

"I'm good," I said. "Thanks again for your help."

After introducing Lydia to Dolores I moved back into the traffic lane. "I'd like to find Deacon," I said. See if he's figured out whatever has been bugging him about the murders. He said he'd get back to us about that, but he hasn't."

"Good idea. You know, I haven't been able to get the picture of Cat's body out of my head. I can't help thinking she may have been raped by whoever killed her. Did Detective Johnson mention anything about that to you?"

"No, but I wondered too when I saw the body."

We looked for Deacon at Drop-in, Koinonia, and the lot and stopped by his pad. No luck.

* * *

As Jackie finished Sunday dinner preparations the next day, I played hide and seek with Andy. While he counted to twenty in the kitchen, I hid behind the dining room door. A

few minutes later Andy yelled, "Found you, Daddy. My turn
to hide."

"You're in big trouble," I said, "because you found a
troll." I snatched him up and moved into the living room
where we began to wrestle on the floor. Just then, the front
doorbell rang.

Andy jumped up and ran to the screen door. "Lydia,
Lydia!" he shouted. "Daddy, Daddy, Lydia's here."

"Tell her to come in, Andy," I said, getting up from the
floor.

"You can come in, Lydia. What did you bring me?" Lydia
sometimes gave Andy small gifts when she saw him—a buf-
falo-head nickel once and a key chain puzzle another time.

Lydia walked in and bent down to give Andy a kiss. "Hi,
Andy. Sounded like you were beating up on a bad guy."

"I beat up my daddy. He was pretending to be a troll.
What did you bring me?"

Lydia stood in the front hall, brow furrowed, scratching
her chin. "Let me see. Did I bring something for my little
buddy? Hmmm."

"Lydia!" said Andy, stomping his foot.

"Oh, now I remember." She reached into her pocket and
withdrew a lucky rabbit's foot with a small chain on it. She
handed it to Andy.

"What is it?"

"It's a rabbit's foot. It's supposed to bring you good
luck."

As Andy raced off to the kitchen to show his mom, Lydia
said to me, "Just in case divine providence isn't enough."

Andy came running back a moment later, followed by
Jackie who gave Lydia a hug.

"How is the *dominee's* wife?" Lydia asked.

Jackie laughed. "You're Polish Catholic. How do you
know the Dutch word for clergyman?"

"Didn't Rob tell you my late husband was Christian Reformed? At any rate, I trust you're being a good *dominee's* wife, stifling all those impulses to have a life of your own, be your own person, all that nasty feminist stuff?"

Jackie laughed again. "Come off it. I know you're a Women's Libber at heart."

After dinner and cleanup, Andy and Jackie went upstairs for naps. Lydia and I sat in the living room, drinking coffee.

"Have you seen anything more of Arnold?" asked Lydia.

"Not since the night he came to my office and wanted his knife back. How about you?"

She shook her head. "Apparently none of the kids have seen him since then, except for Lawton catching him behind the Ministry that time. Have you had any more thoughts on whether he could be the murderer?"

"It's possible, but I'm not sure he's got it together enough to pull off two murders."

Lydia pursed her lips, then said, "He got you to take him for a drive in the wee hours. And sometimes he seems to function pretty well."

"That's true."

Lydia stifled a small burp. "Pardon me. Any possibility Van Boven could have done it, despite his denials?"

"Possible." I shared Brandon's theory. "Johnson said Van Boven's wife vouched for his being home the nights of the murders, but Johnson suspects she would say anything her husband wanted her to."

Lydia looked thoughtful. "To change the subject, Nathan called me this morning. Said Dirk from the gas station went off on Red Feather last night. Red Feather stopped in to buy cigarettes and told Dirk he'd get further in life if he learned to be a little nicer. Dirk came around the counter, grabbed Red Feather by the throat and started choking him. Fortunately, Harley was in the back, heard the commotion and broke it up."

"Maybe you didn't change the subject. Both Harley and Dirk are really down on the kids. I know Dirk is a pain in the ass, but I didn't know he had such a short fuse. What's his story? Do you know?"

"I've never talked to him," said Lydia. "When Blaine was around he used to talk to Dirk and Harley sometimes. Blaine told me that Dirk is Harley's nephew. I guess Dirk got into some kind of trouble when they lived in Detroit. Harley moved here and brought Dirk with him."

"Know if Dirk had any particular contact with Star or Cat?" I asked.

"I don't know. Seems like there was something. Might be worth checking around. I'll let you know if I hear anything."

I had the feeling Lydia knew more than she was saying. Before I could push her on it, she grabbed her purse and said she had to get going.

* * *

At John Ball Park Zoo the next morning, Andy climbed on the statue of John Ball and then fed the ducks in the pond. Jackie and I could hardly pull him away from the monkey exhibit. I had arranged for Lydia to meet me at the park so we could go together to Cat's funeral in Allegan.

She picked me up in her grey and white, two-door '57 Chevy. The car had been lovingly maintained by her husband, and, since his death, by her brother-in-law. I noticed on the ride to the funeral that my cold was almost gone. I was grateful that it wasn't one of those nasty, hanging-on summer colds. I was hardly aware of my forehead wound.

Some of the Souls came to the funeral, too. It was a small affair at the Goodrich Funeral Home, and Cat's family was aloof toward our Grand Rapids contingent.

Lydia dropped me off at home mid-afternoon, and Jackie greeted me with, "You need to call Detective Johnson. He says it's urgent."

I dialed the number with a mixture of hope and dread. "It's Rob," I said. "What now?"

"Another one of your kids, Lester Den Herder. His mother says his nickname was Deacon."

"Was? He's dead?"

"Yeah. We found his body this morning in Riverside Park."

Deacon, who wanted to volunteer at the Ministry. The guy Nathan thought would be perfect for the drug help team. I wanted to slam the phone against the wall. Somebody out there seemed to think it was okay to kill my kids. I flashed on the words of the guy who painted my car: "You watch over us night people." Fine job I was doing.

"Do you know anything else?"

"He was stabbed—"

I heard a raised voice on the other end of the line, but the words weren't clear. It sounded like Kincaid.

Then Johnson's voice, but he wasn't speaking to me. "Dammit. I'll handle this case—" The rest was muffled, then, to me, "Hold on a minute." There were more muffled exchanges, and then Johnson came back on.

"Like I was saying, he was stabbed several times. Coroner's first take is that the stab wounds appear to be similar to those on the Wynsma girl's body."

"And Van Boven is in the hospital."

"No, he went home yesterday morning. The prosecutor will probably charge him with attempted murder, but he says a statutory rape charge won't stick, and we don't have enough to charge him with the Wynsma girl's murder. We also checked on Arnold again, and his parents said they haven't seen him since Friday morning and have no idea where he is. You got anything for me?"

I couldn't think. "No, I guess not."

"If you get any ideas or have any information regarding Deacon, get a hold of me."

I repeated for Jackie what Johnson had said. I felt drained. I shook myself like a wet dog, as if I could shake off the horror of three murders.

Jackie looked at me, long and hard. I knew what she was thinking. She wanted me away from the danger, but she didn't say anything.

I wanted away from the danger, too. But I knew I would move toward it.

CHAPTER 17

I kissed Jackie good-bye, but it was a one-way kiss. She stood with her hands on her hips. "Why don't your street kids just go back home and get away from all the trouble?"

I suspected she wasn't really talking about the kids. "Most of them can't go back home," I said.

She didn't answer. She knew I was right.

I needed to check on some of my congregation. When I arrived at the Soul's pad, Red Feather opened the door. I saw bruises on his neck. "Hey, Rob," he said in a hoarse whisper.

Most of the gang was there, except for a couple of the guys who were working second shift at a furniture factory. It was a sober group.

Lawton sat on a well-worn easy chair, his injured leg propped on an upside down crate. "Guess you heard about Deacon," he said, shaking a cigarette from the pack and lighting it. "We found out about it when we got back from Cat's funeral. Johnson came by to question us." He indicated with his hand an open space on the couch, and I sat down next to a couple of the girls. Lawton scrubbed his face with his hands. "We figure Deacon's murder has got to be connected to the others. What do you think?"

"Johnson said the stab wounds appear to be like the ones on Star's body. He also told me Deacon's body was found in Riverside Park."

I turned to Red Feather. "Heard about Dirk choking you. How you doing?"

"Okay, but if he done this to me," Red Feather rasped, touching his neck, "he coulda murdered Star and Cat and Deacon We was talkin' about that before you come over."

"I wonder about that, too. Did Dirk have any special contact with the murdered kids that anybody knows about?"

Lawton scowled. "Dirk said some nasty things to Deacon, but the prick's talked that way to all of us at one time or another."

"Anything else?" I asked.

Silence. The girls looked at each other. Then one of them said, "Sometimes Dirk says, um, sexual stuff to us girls."

"If no one else is around, he rubs his crotch and stares at us funny," added the other. Both girls studied the floor.

"What kinds of things does he say?"

The girls said nothing and kept their eyes aimed downward.

"He makes you uncomfortable."

The girls nodded.

"Does he scare you?"

They girls looked at each other and shrugged.

I turned my attention to Red Feather. "Did you tell Johnson about Dirk trying to throttle you?"

Red Feather shook his head.

"Have you considered pressing charges?"

"I don't want to get tied up in that mess in case I have to get back for Granny."

" I think Johnson needs to know about it. I'm going to tell him."

Red Feather shrugged.

At Deacon's pad a little later, Wild Bill and his girl were hanging out with several other heads. Wild Bill sat with his guitar case on his knees, his fingers drumming rapidly on it. I parked on a pillow near the door and we sat in silence for a while.

Then Wild Bill said, "What the hell is going on, Rob? Does somebody want to get rid of all of us? We were talking about going someplace where we'd be safe, but we don't know where to go."

I shrugged, not knowing what to say. I rubbed a couple of fingers lightly across the bandage on my forehead because the wound was beginning to itch. "Deacon told me there was something bugging him about the murders. He said he'd let me know when he checked on some things. Did he mention anything about that?"

They all shook their heads.

"We haven't seen much of him at night for a while," said Wild Bill. "I figured maybe he was spending time with his family."

When I finished talking with the heads, I drove to the police station. I found Johnson sitting behind his desk. He looked disheveled, sport coat wrinkled and tie askew. The big man's shoulders drooped. He appeared to have aged since I'd seen him last. "Number three," he growled, "and we still don't know much of anything. At least Lawton's got an alibi this time."

Kincaid was not at his desk.

"So Deacon was killed in Riverside Park?" I said.

"No. Looks like he was killed somewhere else and dumped there. Maybe the autopsy will shed some light. Any ideas?"

I told Johnson about my meeting with the businessmen who were neighbors of the Street Ministry, what I knew about Harley and Dirk, and that Dirk had attacked Red Feather. I told him that something about the murders had been bugging

Deacon and that he said he would check into it and get back to me.

"Did he get back to you before he was killed?"

"No."

"We'll interview the guys at the gas station along with other business owners in the area. So, most of the businessmen are being more, uh, tolerant toward the kids? Is that what you're saying?"

"All but Harley and Dirk."

"Now I think I understand why the word is out to the uniforms not to, uh, enforce the law so aggressively with your gang rowdies and your druggies. Anyways, get a hold of me if you got anything new."

When I stopped in at the Ministry, Lydia was fuming. She jerked a piece of paper out of her typewriter, balled it up, and threw it in the wastebasket.

"I can't get anything done here." She scowled at me. "Police in and out of here, newspaper and TV people. I wish they'd leave us alone."

I knew that wasn't really what she was upset about.

She reached for a tissue and blew her nose. "Couple of weeks ago, Deacon brought me a bunch of flowers. When I asked him where he got them, he told me I didn't want to know. Probably picked them in the park, the big dummy."

I reached for her hand, but she jerked it away.

"I'm just so mad I could spit nickels. These are our kids and we can't protect them. Some no good so-and-so out there …"

I said nothing, feeling as helpless and angry as Lydia.

"Go on, now. Let me get this typing done."

I went into my office and grabbed my sermon to work on at home where I had my Scripture commentaries and other reference books. I stared out the window for a bit, wishing I could see Star and Cat and Deacon once more, listen to them, give them each a hug. On my way out, I stopped again at Lydia's desk. She had completed typing my report to our supporting churches and pushed it toward me to sign. She looked up at me. "Sorry I was so mean to you before."

"I didn't think you were mean, just angry about the murders and feeling helpless. Same as me."

"I just wish you didn't, we didn't … I mean, stopping murders isn't supposed to be part of our ministry. But somebody's got to … oh, I don't know." She threw up her hands.

After a moment I said, "Lydia, have you had any more thoughts about Harley and Dirk?"

Her eyes narrowed. Her hand rested against the side of her head, her index finger lightly tapping her temple. She'd shifted into her role as Communication Central. "Dirk says something nasty to at least one of the kids every day. Calls them all sorts of terrible names that I'd never repeat. The things he says to some of the girls …" She shook her head.

"Like what, Lydia? I know you don't like to use nasty words, but it might be important."

"He says suggestive things."

"You mean sexually suggestive."

Lydia shifted uncomfortably in her chair. "You have to understand that my generation wasn't brought up to talk about these things. No free love and all that when I was young."

"I know this is hard for you, but try to tell me what you've heard."

"Some of the girls tell me that Dirk offered to give them money if they would do certain, um, sexual things for him."

"Did Star or Cat ever tell you anything like that?"

"Cat did."

"What did she tell you?"

"Dirk said he'd give her a hundred dollars if she let him take pictures of her with her clothes off. He wanted to do it upstairs at the gas station." Lydia studied her typewriter.

"What did Cat say to him?"

"She said no, of course. Actually she told him to, um, go do it to himself."

"Blaine told me that Dirk and Harley sometimes have a few guys in that upper room to play cards at night, but I never would have guessed anything like you're talking about went on up there. Did you tell the detectives this?"

"I didn't think it was connected to the murders. I remembered this yesterday at your place, but I didn't want to talk about it."

"I understand."

Thinking about what Lydia had said, I left the building and walked into the station next door. There were no customers and Dirk was lounging on a chair in front of a fan. My car was due for an oil change.

"Hey, Dirk. How's it going?"

He looked at something on the wall over my left shoulder and grunted. It was hot and humid, and he had taken off his shirt, which hung on the back of his chair. He wore a dirty white undershirt. I'd not noticed before how muscular his upper body was. He tipped his baseball cap to the side.

"I hear another kid got it," he said.

"Were you here late last night? See anything unusual?"

"Nope." He lit a cigarette.

I gathered he was going be his usual chatty self. "Think you'd have time to change the oil in my car tomorrow?"

"Yup," he said blowing out smoke, now finding something of interest over my right shoulder.

"What time should I bring it in?"

"After lunch."

I wasn't going to get anything more from him.

* * *

During supper Jackie was frosty and said little to me. As I told her about Dirk and Harley, I was careful how I put things in front of Andy. I told her I was having Dirk change the oil in the car the next day.

At that, she looked up and said sharply, "Couldn't you have that done someplace else?"

I'd walked into that one.

"It's not like I'll be taking a risk by getting the oil changed there," I said.

"It's just another excuse to play detective, Robert."

"Why are you calling Daddy Robert, Mama?"

"I like to call him that sometimes, Andy. Just like Grandma Vander Laan does."

"But Grandma only calls him Robert when she's mad at him. Are you mad at Daddy?"

Jackie looked at me, then back at Andy. "Yes, I am mad at Daddy, but this is between your dad and me. Now I don't want you to interrupt us. It's not about you. Okay?"

"Okay, Mama." He looked like he might cry.

"I know you're mad at me, Jacks," I said, "but I have a hunch that we may finally be on the right track here. I told Johnson all about it. I'm not putting myself in any jeopardy." I sneaked a glance at Andy, not putting it past him to understand what I was talking about. "If I learn anything, I'll pass it on to Johnson."

I could see that Jackie was not mollified.

"By the way," said Jackie, "my mom's picking Andy up tomorrow morning and taking him to the farm for the day instead of watching him here."

After supper I suggested we all walk to the park. Jackie asked if I'd go alone with Andy.

When Andy and I got back home, I gave him a bath and put him to bed. Jackie left, saying she was going to visit with Blaine's wife and a couple of other women friends. The four of them had been getting together for a few months, reading and discussing Betty Friedan's *The Feminine Mystique*, trying to figure out what feminism meant in their lives. As a result of those discussions I was spending more time doing household tasks and child care. I was pretty sure more changes were coming. As Jackie went out the door, she said she wanted to talk to someone she wasn't mad at. I was grateful that she had a solid support group, but I wished I could be a fly on the wall.

I sat on the front steps as darkness gathered. The street was quiet. I heard occasional traffic on Eastern Avenue, half a block away. I thought about Van Boven. Could he pull off the murder of Cat so soon after being wounded by Lawton? Could he have killed Deacon because he had a taste for it, like Brandon figured? My thoughts turned to Arnold, and I wondered about his disappearance? Then I tried to picture Dirk committing the murders. What kind of trouble had he been in before? If Dirk was the murderer, did Harley know about it? Was Harley in on it? Had Harley and Dirk hatched their own diabolical scheme to clean up the streets of Grand Rapids?

I remembered what Lydia had said about Dirk wanting to take pictures of Cat. I thought about the upstairs room at the station. I wondered if Cat or Star had ever been up there. What about Deacon? What would entice the kids to go up there? Money? Or in Deacon's case, looking for evidence of the murders?

After almost being killed by Van Boven and trying to numb myself with alcohol, I had been ready to give up on solving the murders. Sober, I realized I had to do what I could. My congregation included kids who had been dealt a tough hand and were scorned by straight society. They were kids I'd come to love.

I went back inside the house, poured myself a glass of iced tea and picked up the *Times* from the coffee table. A photo of Deacon stared at me from the front page along with the headline, THIRD DOWNTOWN MURDER. I read Stu Peterson's story and noted that Deacon's father had died four years earlier. The funeral for Deacon would be held on Thursday.

After finding a listing in the phone book, I decided to try the number. Deacon's mother answered. I introduced myself and expressed my sympathy. I told her about my recent conversation with Deacon, when he said he wanted to help at the Ministry. With a grief-choked voice she thanked me for calling. I said I'd see her at the funeral.

I didn't notice the gathering storm until a clap of thunder startled me so much I nearly dropped the phone.

CHAPTER 18

"**M**y sister says she'd be glad to talk to her husband if you're interested in a call to Jamestown." Jackie's mom had arrived to pick up Andy to take him to the farm. Her sister and brother-in-law were members of the Jamestown church where he was an elder. Mom was back on the familiar parental theme. I knew the intensity of her urging this morning came largely from the news about the latest murder.

I decided to close the door firmly. "Thanks for your concern, but I'm not interested."

"You sure? You have to think of your fam—"

"I'm sure."

Mom's shoulders heaved, accompanied by a soft sigh.

I walked outside with her and Andy and put the butterfly net in the back seat of her car. Andy was, as usual, excited to go to the farm.

I mowed the lawn, then cleaned the garage, keeping a promise I'd made to Jackie a few months earlier. After a shower and lunch, I drove downtown and parked on the street near the gas station since all the customer spots were full. Dirk and Harley were both at the gas pumps, so I went inside to wait for them and give them my car key.

I needed to use the restroom and was washing my hands when I heard Harley and Dirk's voices coming through a vent near the ceiling. Their office was on the other side of the wall. Dirk sounded like he was complaining, but I couldn't make out all the words.

Harley's words were clear. "Stop whining about that fucking hippie. The town's better off without him. Now get your ass back out to the pumps."

Holy shit! What did that mean? Was it just their usual badmouthing of the kids? If Dirk was complaining, was he accusing Harley of something? I thought I'd heard Dirk say, "You shouldn't have …" Shouldn't have what? I stared at the vent, hoping to hear more.

Maybe my imagination was working overtime, but my skin crawled and my shoulders were scrunched as if to ward off a blow.

I wanted to get out of the bathroom without being seen. What would I say if I ran into Harley or Dirk? I was frozen with indecision. A bell rang—the one that sounded when a vehicle passed over the hose by the pumps. Maybe they were both back out at the pumps. Or maybe not.

God, help me, I prayed, as I unlocked the door and walked out.

Dirk and Harley were both outside, pumping gas for customers. I walked out the front door toward my car, then turned around and went back into the station. I tossed my keys on the counter and turned to walk back out, almost bumping into Harley.

"Keys are on the counter," I said. Before he could say anything, I asked, "Did you hear about Deacon's death?"

Harley's eyes narrowed. "I can see someone wanting those hoodlums off the streets. I haven't made a secret of how I feel about them, but killing them is something else. I figured it was one of the gang kids who did it, but three murders? Man, I just don't know." He moved around the counter and put money in the till

He sat down behind the counter, tipping the chair back against the wall. I was going to ask him if he knew Deacon and what he thought of him, but he barely paused for breath. "What bugs me is all these cops and TV people going into your place and half of them parking in our spots here. We finally get you guys trained not to park here, and now this circus."

At that moment Dirk walked in and put money in the cash register.

"We were just talking about Deacon's murder," I said. "That's three of the kids now, Dirk."

Dirk looked at the floor, hands stuffed in his pockets. Nothing unusual about his behavior.

I let the silence hang there, pretending to pay attention to Dirk while watching Harley out of the corner of my eye. Harley squirmed in his chair and tapped his right foot rapidly. Then, in one fluid motion, he banged the chair down to the floor and stood up. "Can't just stand around here shooting the breeze all day. If I'm not mistaken, Dirk's changing the oil in your car."

As I left I noticed a police car pulling in across the street. Johnson and Kincaid got out. Johnson shot a glance in my direction and Kincaid waved to me before they went into the camera store. Probably interviewing area businessmen. I should have mentioned to Johnson that Brandon was on our board and alerted Brandon to the police visit.

When I entered the Ministry, Lydia said, "Sit." I turned a chair around, straddled it, my arms resting on the back of the chair. "I've been thinking since we talked yesterday," she said. "That time Cat talked to me about Dirk was right about when Lawton was busted for fighting in the park. The charge was later dropped. That was close to the end of last month. I woke up with that on my mind this morning and I can't shake it."

She looked at me like I was supposed to know what she meant. Funny thing was, I did. Almost. It felt like missing a butterfly with Andy's net. I started thinking out loud. "Lawton gets busted for aggravated assault. Dirk asks Cat to pose for pictures. Offers her a hundred bucks. She refuses." I snapped my fingers. "Do you remember when Lawton got out?"

Lydia's eyes narrowed. "I think it was just a day or two after he was arrested."

"Was he released on his own recognizance?"

"No. Lawton told me that he'd jumped bond once before, so they made him post bail."

"How did he come up with bail money?"

"Hmm," said Lydia, eyes widening. "None of the Souls were working at that time. Oh, wait a minute. Red Feather was working. He probably came up with the money."

"I don't think so. His grandmother was sick and I know he was sending her money."

"You're right. Do you think Cat could have changed her mind about posing so she could bail Lawton out?"

"Maybe. And what about Star? Any reason she'd have posed for Dirk?"

Lydia shrugged.

"Ten to one says Lawton's bail was a thousand dollars," I said.

"So Cat would have needed a hundred?"

"Bingo."

"Let's check with Lawton about his bail," Lydia said, a steely determination in her eyes.

Before I had a chance to tell her what I'd overheard at the gas station, Johnson and Kincaid walked in, and I stood to greet them. "What's up, Detectives?"

"Could we talk privately, Rob?" asked Johnson. Looking at Lydia he added, "I don't mean to be rude, ma'am."

"We can do that," I said, "but Lydia and I just came up with an idea on the case. You want to hear that first, or you want to talk privately first?"

"What you got?"

Lydia told the detectives that Cat might have posed for Dirk to raise Lawton's bail.

Johnson frowned. "I don't think I have enough on the gas station guys to get a search warrant. By the way, Rob, I saw you coming from over there a few minutes ago. You weren't sniffing for clues, were you?"

"Just having my oil changed," I said. I told him what I'd overheard in the restroom. "I did notice Harley getting nervous when I mentioned Deacon's death."

"What a relief to know you aren't playing detective," Johnson said with a scowl.

Lydia sat up straighter and looked Johnson in the eye. "Excuse my saying so, young man, but there have been three murders of our kids. You need all the help you can get."

Johnson, to his credit, looked directly at Lydia and said, "Ma'am, I'm sorry. You're absolutely right. We do need all the help we can get." He reached into his pocket and took out two of his cards. He wrote his home number on them and handed one to me and one to Lydia. "If either of you thinks of anything else, you get a hold of me, day or night."

Lydia lifted her chin a notch. "Thank you, Detective. I will."

Johnson, Kincaid and I moved into my office and I closed the door.

Johnson looked out the window. "Whew. That woman is something else. Not many folks talk to me like that when I'm on official business. Come to think of it, only my mother and the chief talk to me like that."

I glanced at Kincaid. Small muscle movements around the younger detective's eyes and mouth made it look like it was an effort for him to wear a sober face.

Johnson turned to me. "I'll find out about Lawton's bail, the amount and date it was posted, and who posted it. Although, you'll probably find out all that before I do." Johnson's bushy eyebrows lifted. He shifted his bulk in the chair. "There's one thing that's a little different about Deacon's murder. We're keeping this under wraps, but I want your reaction. I know you're used to keeping things confidential," he said, a trace of sarcasm in his voice. "You already know Deacon was stabbed—several times in the chest and abdomen, like the Wynsma girl. The confidential part is that his throat was cut from behind, and there was a note pinned to his shirt. It said, 'No gang member, but still a lost soul.'"

I gave an involuntary shudder. "The murderer wants to send a message."

"Yeah. Any ideas?"

I rubbed a hand over my eyes. "The murderer might be saying these kids are lost souls, just trash. He's cleaning up the streets of Grand Rapids. Maybe a message to other downtown kids, that anyone of them could be next."

"Kincaid and I are thinking pretty much along the same lines."

I looked at Kincaid who, by the downturn of his mouth and his furrowed brow, appeared to be registering his usual disapproval of Johnson sharing information with me.

"Anyways," Johnson went on, "I dug up a little on Harley Scanlon and Dirk Boyle. They're both from Chicago. Scanlon's brother is Boyle's old man, and he's doing time for murder. Boyle and Scanlon moved from Chicago to Detroit where Boyle's got a sheet. Arrested twice for assault. Suspect in the case of a murdered girl, but they couldn't get anything on him. That one's still unsolved. Boyle was also a suspect in an arson case. All around, a nice family. They moved here three years ago."

"Anything else?"

"We'll interview them at the station when we leave here. On a brighter note, Van Boven was charged yesterday for assault with intent to commit murder for his little rumble with you at the gravel pit. Prosecutor decided not to include the statutory rape charge. And Arnold's in P.R." Pine Rest was the local Christian psychiatric hospital.

"Rob, use discretion," said Kincaid. "If Scanlon or Boyle are guilty of homicide and they suspect you heard something incriminating while you were in the lavatory, remember that 'discretion is the better part of valor.'"

Fancy talk and quoting Shakespeare. If his parents talked that way, it would be normal for him. Still, he must be aware of how his fellow officers viewed him. Maybe his attitude was: This is me, like it or lump it. I could admire that.

Johnson grunted. "And watch your back."

As soon as the detectives left the building, Lydia appeared at my office door and gave me a conspiratorial look. "So what did I miss?"

I filled her in on what Sid had told me about Harley and Dirk and about Van Boven being charged, but nothing about the note pinned to Deacon's body or his throat being cut.

Lydia gave me a hard look. She knew I wasn't telling her everything.

"So, you ready to hit the streets with me again tonight?" I asked.

"Darn tootin'."

After a half hour of deskwork, I called Jackie's mom and said I'd come to pick up Andy and save her a trip into town.

I needed to get my car, so I headed over to the station with a queasy feeling in my stomach and sweaty palms.

There were no customers at the pumps. When I entered the station, Harley was pacing the small area behind the counter. "Stupid cops took Dirk to the station for questioning just because he tried to teach that gang punk some manners. Had to finish your car myself."

I almost told Harley I was sorry about that, but it would not have been the truth.

After I paid my bill, Harley came around the counter. He positioned himself between the door and me and looked at me sharply. "When you dropped off your car, Dirk says he saw you come out of the station while him and me were at the pumps, then go back in and drop your key on the counter. Were you in the john before that?"

Shit. I thought of Sam telling Lydia that they needed to teach me how to lie better.

"I came in as you were heading out to the pumps, started to come out to give you the key, then decided to just drop it on the counter. Why?"

Harley's eyes narrowed. "Just wondered."

I started to step around him, but he moved to block my exit.

"You wouldn't lie about a little thing like using my bathroom, would you?"

I attempted a look of bafflement. "Why would I?"

Driving out of the city, I gradually released the tension from my encounter with Harley while listening to the latest hits.

As I walked from my car to the back door at the farm, the smell of freshly baked bread along with the sound of "truly Christian radio," wafted into the yard. I knocked, called a greeting and walked in. Jackie's mom was in the kitchen beginning preparations for supper.

She brushed her hands on her apron and greeted me warmly with a hug and a smile. She appeared to hold no hard feelings regarding my rejection of her suggestion about the Jamestown church. I went down the basement to say hello to Jackie's dad.

He looked up from cleaning his twelve-gauge pump shot gun, the one I used when I hunted with him and Jackie.

"*Hoe ist er mee, jonge?*" How are you, young man? It was a greeting I'd often heard growing up.

"I'm hanging in there."

We talked about the fall hunting season. Then he asked, "Will you and Jackie come out a few times to hunt?"

"I hope so. You know Jackie. She wouldn't miss it." Jackie had started hunting in junior high when she realized it was a good way to connect with her dad.

He asked about the latest murder and the progress of the investigation. I told him of the latest developments. Wrinkling his brow, he looked into the distance. "Wasn't Van Boven on your short list of suspects?" he said. "What do you think now?"

"He was on my short list, sort of. Although, at that time I didn't know for sure if he was the neighbor who molested Star." I told him Brandon's theory regarding Van Boven being the murderer.

"I'm more interested in what you think."

"It's possible Brandon is right, but Deacon was killed just a couple of nights after Van Boven got his skull creased by a bullet and injured some ribs. I wonder if he'd be recovered enough to be off on another murder escapade so soon? I haven't ruled him out, but Dirk from the gas station is at the top of my list now." I told my father-in-law my suspicion that the girls had agreed to let Dirk take nude photos of them.

He laid the barrel of the shotgun on the workbench and placed a hand on my shoulder. "It's one thing to use your brain to try to figure out who the murderer is, but I don't like you poking into this investigation as if you're a cop. You're lucky that you weren't injured any worse in this business with Van Boven."

I wondered if he, too, was going to get on my case about leaving the Street Ministry, but he said nothing more.

He put the gun together and hung it below the others in the cabinet. After he locked it we walked upstairs. Andy and

I said good-bye and headed for home with a freshly-baked loaf of bread, the smell making me drool.

When we got back home, I took my sermon folder from the car and put it in the file drawer of my desk, determined to do some more work on it the next day before going to the office.

During supper Jackie expressed her amusement that Lydia was continuing to accompany me on night ministry. "I just hope I'm that cool and energetic when I'm seventy," she said. "By the way, did my mom talk to you about Jamestown?"

"Yes, and I told her that I'm definitely not interested."

Jackie scowled.

"Your dad asked if we were planning to do some hunting with him again this fall. I told him we hoped to get out a few times."

"I've been thinking of taking a week off during hunting season and staying at the farm."

"What do you mean?" I said, my voice sharper than I'd intended. "We always coordinate our vacation times so we can travel and tent camp."

"I'm just thinking about it."

CHAPTER 19

Lawton roared into the lot on his Harley, apparently having recovered it from the gravel pit. Several gang members piled out of Mad Dog's old Ford station wagon. The kids were still not used to seeing Lydia on the street with me and gathered around to talk with her.

"Where's the rest of the gang tonight?" asked Lydia.

"A few of the guys decided to split for a while," said Mad Dog.

I wasn't surprised some of the kids had left town. I wondered if others were considering it. I stepped over to Lawton who was climbing off his bike. I asked him how he'd come up with the money for his bail earlier in the summer.

Lawton wrinkled his brow. "Cat came up with the hundred bucks for the bail agent." Lydia joined us as Lawton continued. "Let's see. Cat said she seen her dad in town and he wanted to help her out. I figured it was lucky timing."

"Lydia, want to tell Lawton what Cat told you?"

Lydia repeated her story about Dirk proposing the photo session.

Lawton's eyes turned cold. "That piece of shit. I'd like to kick his sorry ass."

I touched his arm. "I know you would, Lawton. But we have to be cool about this. If he's the murderer, we don't want to do anything to blow the investigation."

"So we're supposed to sit on our asses and not do a fuckin' thing?"

"For now, let's keep our eyes and ears open," I said. "Johnson and Kincaid really want to crack this case."

"Red Feather was the only one workin' when I got busted. He was sendin' most of his money to his grandma. The gang started scrapin' the bottom of the barrel after that, and Star said she thought she could get some money from an aunt. You think Star posed for Dirk, too?"

"Let's suppose she did," I said. "And let's suppose Dirk took the photos upstairs at the station. Why would she be killed at the apartment?"

Lawton shook his head. "I guess she could have had Dirk take her there. But I don't know why she wouldn't just join the rest of us in the lot or at Drop-in."

As the three of us walked to the Ministry, I told Lawton about the conversation fragment I'd overheard at the gas station and my fear that Harley might suspect I'd been eavesdropping.

"Sure as hell sounds like they was talkin' about Deacon's murder," said Lawton.

Lydia nodded.

Their take on it reinforced my own suspicions.

At the Ministry Lawton strolled into Drop-in. Lydia smiled broadly at Nathan who was seated at the front desk. "Hey, you look good in my spot. Maybe I should take up your lawn care job, and you can be Communication Central for a while."

"Oh, Lydia, I could never replace you. But I'm sure you could mow lawns as well as I do."

"You old brown-noser."

"So, you're really getting into doing street ministry with the Reverend, eh?" said Nathan. "Straighten out any bad guys tonight, or too busy keeping Rob on the straight and narrow?"

Lydia laughed. "You got it." Then, saying she was going to check something with Lawton, she, too, moved into Drop-in.

"Have you picked up any scuttlebutt from the kids about Deacon's murder?" I asked Nathan.

"Nada. They're really blown away by it."

We were discussing how the kids were handling the murders and how else we might help them when Johnson and Kincaid entered the building.

"Lydia with you tonight, Rob?" asked Johnson.

I pointed a thumb toward Drop-in.

"Can we talk with both of you for a few minutes?"

The detectives and I headed toward my office, and I signaled Lydia to join us.

When we were seated Johnson said, "Couldn't get a warrant to search the station. Judge told me we needed more evidence. His exact words were, 'Can't go searching the places of everyone who'd like to see the gang and dopers off the streets. You'd have to start with my place.'"

I grimaced.

Kincaid leaned forward. "We did take Mr. Dirk Boyle in for questioning today regarding his assault on Red Feather."

"Harley told me. Question him about the murders, too?"

Kincaid leaned back in his chair and, after a pause, said, "Yes." Then he was quiet. I was surprised he'd volunteered that much.

I looked at Johnson, my face a question mark.

"Boyle's so shifty," he said, "it's hard to tell, but I think he's hiding something. Red Feather refuses to press charges against Boyle for attacking him, so we had nothing to hold Boyle on. Red Feather claimed he didn't want to be tied down having to testify in case he had to go out of State to see an ailing grandmother."

"She raised him," I said, "and they're very close. We've got something else for you," I added, changing the subject. "Found out that Cat claimed she got Lawton's bail money from her father, but we still think she got it posing for Dirk."

"I said you'd find out about that before I did. Anyways, I'll contact her father and see if he gave her the money. If Cat did get the money from Dirk, would she lie about it to the other gang members?"

Lydia's eyes were troubled. "Yes, I think she would. When she told me about Dirk's proposition, the idea was repulsive to her." She turned to me. "I didn't tell you this before, Rob, but I realize now it might be important. Cat said Dirk wanted to, um, play with himself while he watched her touch herself." She gave a small shudder. "That's what really turned her off, but I think getting Lawton out of jail might have won out over her revulsion. If it did, I think she'd be ashamed of how she got the money."

I shared with Johnson our hunch that Star may have wanted to raise food money for the gang the same way Cat raised the bail money.

"Speaking of the Wynsma girl," said Johnson, "the toxicology report showed that her body had an extremely high alcohol content."

Kincaid shifted uneasily.

"If Dirk murdered Star," I mused, " maybe he got her drunk before taking pictures of her."

Lydia frowned. "And if Star was ashamed of what she was doing, maybe she wanted to numb herself before she posed for Dirk."

"If Star was totally wasted," I said, "Dirk might have brought her home, found the apartment empty and killed her there. But why?"

Johnson didn't say anything. Kincaid wrote furiously in his notebook.

I told the detectives about being confronted by Harley who was probably worried I'd overheard something while I was in his restroom.

Lydia threw up her hands. "It's just so gol-darned frustrating the killer hasn't been arrested. We're really scared another one of the kids …" Her voice trailed off.

"Yeah." Johnson's chair scraped the floor as he stood up. "We better go follow up on some things."

I walked with the detectives down the front steps. Lydia joined me on the street a moment later, and we walked past the gas station, which was closed. Our eyes went to the darkened upstairs windows and the outside stairs. "Looks like nothing's going on up there tonight," I said. "I sure would like to get a look, but I guess we'll have to leave that to Johnson. I mean, if we're on the right track, evidence could be anywhere, but I've got a strong feeling about that room."

"Detective Johnson can't get a search warrant," said Lydia. "How long do we dare wait?"

"I know what you mean," I said as we boarded Night Watch, "but what can we do?"

"A lot. I bumped into Sam downtown today, and we had lunch. We came up with an idea about how to get a look at that upper room. She isn't working tonight. I just called her from the front desk, and she'll meet us at the Windmill Cafe. She said she's way ahead of us, whatever that means."

And I thought I had the detective bug.

On the drive over I tried to quiz Lydia about the idea she and Sam had come up with, but she just made a zipping motion across her lips. I followed her into the restaurant where Sam waited, wearing a short white skirt and a low-cut light blue top. The waitress brought us coffee.

"So," said Sam, chin propped on her fists, elbows resting on the table, "It's all set for tonight. Did you tell Rob our plan, Lydia?"

Lydia looked surprised. "But it was just an idea."

"Yeah, I know, but I decided to check things out, and Dirk wants to take pictures of me tonight. I got gas there this afternoon and flirted with him. Then I came back later with some car trouble I finagled. Seriously, it helps to have a brother who's a mechanic. Dirk took the bait. He offered me a hundred and fifty bucks for a photo session. He's expecting me to meet him upstairs at the gas station at ten forty-five."

I scowled and shook my head. "What the heck are you talking about?"

"The idea," said Lydia, "was that Sam would seduce Dirk into proposing a photo session. As soon as Sam joined Dirk in the upper room, Lawton would break in downstairs and make some noise. Then you and I, Rob, would run upstairs to alert Dirk to the break-in, in case he didn't come to check it out. That would give Sam time for a fast look around. Then Sam would skedaddle out of there, and we'd pick her up."

I turned to Sam. "Lydia told me you were way ahead of us. I guess you are."

Sam flashed a grin.

Lydia's eyes were shining with excitement. "Are you sure you're all right with this Sam? It could be risky."

Sam laughed. "I live for danger!"

I shook my head, but I was catching up. "It just might work. We've got to check with Lawton. If we can't find him or he won't do it—"

"Oh, he'll do it," said Lydia. "He told me a few minutes ago that he feels terrible because his getting arrested for assault may have been the reason Cat agreed to pose for Dirk. Plus, he'd been thinking about quitting the gang and settling down with Cat, but he hadn't worked up the nerve to talk to her about it. Before I left Drop-in I told him to stick around in case we needed him later."

My attention returned to Sam. "You're going to be our eyes in that room, Sam. Take in as much detail as you can, but getting out safely is the most important thing. Do you understand?"

"Got it."

"Let me ask you something. Why are you willing to risk this? Aside from 'living for danger?'"

"I think Dirk is taking advantage of these girls. And maybe he murdered them. Let's just say that I know a little about being taken advantage of. You helped me learn that I can talk about my problems. Remember when you bugged me to talk to a counselor? I'm seeing one at school, and I guess, I don't know, I sort of want to give something back."

I didn't know what to say as I looked at Lydia and Sam and thought about Lawton. I breathed a prayer of thanks for our motley detective crew.

A short time later, Lydia and I found Lawton hanging out in the parking lot, and he readily agreed to participate in our scheme. A few minutes before Sam's appointment with Dirk, Lydia and I sat parked across from the station. The lights were off downstairs, but an outline of light shone around windows darkened by shades or curtains in the upper room.

The door to the upstairs room opened and a man, presumably Dirk, stepped out to the top of the stairs. In the dim light, we couldn't see him clearly. When he came part way down and looked around, Lydia and I slid down in our seats. The man appeared to look at his watch, then across Jefferson toward where we sat in the car, then toward the Ministry next door. Nobody was on the street. He turned and walked back up the stairs and closed the door.

We waited. Suddenly, Sam was standing by Lydia's open window. Without looking at us she said, "This Lawton guy ready to go?"

"He sure is," said Lydia.

"Then wish me luck, guys." Sam headed across the street.

I clutched the steering wheel with both hands.

Lydia reached over and touched my arm. "Relax. Remember that Sam worked the street. She knows how to handle herself."

I loosened my death grip on the steering wheel.

Sam reached the top of the stairs and knocked on the door. The door opened. Sam went inside. The door closed.

Lydia and I waited, straining to hear a noise from Lawton's break-in. I saw a dark movement inside the station and then heard a crash.

Lydia yelled, "Hey, I think somebody broke into the station! I heard a noise!"

We jumped out of the car and ran across the street and up the stairs, yelling for Dirk and Harley. We almost bumped into Dirk as he stepped out, closing the door behind him.

Lydia and I backed down a couple of steps to give him room on the landing. "Someone just broke into the station," I said.

"I thought I heard a noise. One of those damn Lost Souls, I bet." Dirk glared. "I better take a look."

We descended the stairs slowly because Lydia was leading the way, taking the steps like an old lady. Good. Give Sam a few more seconds. We went around to the front of the station. Dirk unlocked the door, and we followed him inside. He turned the lights on. The chair behind the counter was overturned. The cash register lay on the floor, the drawer open, a few bills and some change scattered around. Dirk grunted as he put the heavy register back on the counter. He gathered the money and counted it.

"Funny. It's all here," he said.

"Whoever broke in must have taken off when I yelled," offered Lydia.

We followed Dirk into the office where he opened and closed the drawers in the desk. Next he checked the area of the station where the cars were worked on. He looked around and was apparently satisfied that tools and parts lay undisturbed. Broken glass was scattered on the floor beneath an open window.

"Want us to call the police?" I asked, trying to be helpful.

Dirk swore under his breath. "Nah, nothin' taken."

Not even call the police to report it? He must have wanted to get back upstairs fast.

Dirk closed the window.

"Let me put something over that broken window for you?" I said.

"Nah. I'll take care of it."

Lydia tried another tack. "If you'd like, Dirk, I could call Harley for you while you board up that window."

"Nah. I'll call him. You guys take off. I got it from here."

Lydia made one last attempt. "Why don't you let me at least sweep up that broken glass for you?"

"I got it! You guys bug off now!"

We couldn't stretch it any further. I hoped it was enough. Lydia and I walked out the door and stood outside talking, not wanting to get into my car and drive away too quickly. We could see Dirk moving efficiently to clean up so he could get back upstairs.

Sam had a couple more minutes, at most.

CHAPTER 20

Sam flew down the steps from the upper room, carrying something. Evidence of the murders?

I eased away from the curb as we watched her run into the shadows of the alley. I drove around the block and pulled up by the curb. Lawton climbed aboard. I was about to jump out and tear up the alley to find Sam when she appeared, hopping on one foot and putting on a shoe. She'd been carrying her shoes, not evidence to nail Dirk. I felt a ripple of disappointment followed by a wave of relief that she was okay. She joined Lawton in the back seat.

I drove a block before she let out a whoosh of air and said, "Thank God I'm out of there!"

Then everyone started talking at once, draining off the tension. Lydia finally thought to introduce Sam and Lawton.

I parked in front of the Windmill Cafe, and we chose a booth as far as possible from the few other customers. After the waitress brought our coffee and pops, we looked expectantly at Sam.

"Well." Sam drew out the word, still a little breathless. "When I got up there, Dirk wanted to start taking pictures right away. I asked him if he could get me something to drink first, and he got me a beer from a refrigerator. Then I asked him if he'd ever done this before. He said it was a hobby of his." Sam shivered. "The whole time he leered at me and rubbed his crotch. Seriously, I've met a few creepy guys, but that guy is off-the-scale creepy."

"Did he use an instant camera or did he have professional equipment?" I asked.

"He had a camera already set up on a tripod. Some lights on poles, a plain backdrop hung behind the couch. Looked more professional than I expected. When he said he wanted to get started, I told him I had to see the hundred and fifty first. It's hard to take much time counting seven twenties and a ten." Sam laughed. "But I dropped a couple of bills and started over to give Lawton more time. I figured if Dirk was content looking down my front for a minute, he wouldn't notice I was stalling. I was pretty nervous. I mean, I was afraid I might screw things up for you guys. Plus, if he murdered other girls …"

"What did the room look like?" I asked.

Sam described a clean room with a comfortable couch and chairs, mirrors on two of the walls, a few cupboards, card table and folding chairs leaning against one wall, men's magazines on tables, a refrigerator, black shades on the windows.

"What happened next?" I asked.

Sam took a drink of her pop. "I put the money in the pocket of my skirt and said I was ready. Dirk told me to lean over the coffee table first. As I bent over to put my beer down on the table, I let my hair hide my face. He took a few shots. Then he unzipped his pants." She shuddered again. "The creep has pictures of me."

Lydia placed a hand on Sam's arm.

"Then we heard noises downstairs. Seriously, your timing was perfect, Lawton. We heard you guys hollering, and Dirk told me to go into the bathroom and wait for him to check things out. Oh, I forgot that. There's a bathroom up there. I went in and kept the door open a crack. When you guys and Dirk went down the steps, I checked the bathroom first. Then I tried the cupboards in the main room. All I found was a big reel of film in one of those cans and a movie camera. The film can was sealed, and the movie camera looked pretty snazzy. Most of the cupboards were bare, like they weren't used or were cleaned out recently. There was a door to a room behind one of the mirrors. I tried it, but it was locked. I left the money he gave me on the coffee table. Figured he'd think I chickened out."

I frowned. "A door to a room behind a mirror. Could it have been a two-way mirror?"

Sam's eyes went big. "You mean like a mirror you can see through from the other side? Oh, cripes! You think someone could have been in there?"

"I don't know, but it would be best if you're not seen anywhere near the station for a while."

We sat in silence. After a few minutes Sam's eyes began to tear. "I screwed up, didn't I?"

The rest of us all objected at once and tried to reassure her. "Sam," I said, "you did everything we hoped. It's not your fault you didn't find incriminating evidence."

We trooped out of the restaurant and piled into my car. I dropped Lawton off at the lot. After dropping Sam at her car, I followed her to make sure she got home safely. Since Lydia and I were both too depressed to do any more night ministry, I took her home.

As I drove back to my place, I hoped Jackie wouldn't awaken when I came to bed. I dreaded talking with her about the night. I was thoroughly bummed about our amateurish detective work. I'd been so sure we'd find something to prove Dirk was the murderer.

Driving south on Eastern I glanced in my mirror to see a flashing light. I pulled over and waited while a police car went by. I stretched and yawned, then pulled back into the traffic lane.

As I neared my house, I saw flashers. I felt a chill. A police car blocked my street. I parked on Eastern and ran toward my house. A uniformed officer at the intersection put out a hand to stop me. "Sorry, Father. We're keeping spectators away from the fire."

I craned my neck to look around him. "Which house? Which house? I live on this street!"

"Oh, sorry, Father. I didn't know. Go ahead. Just don't interfere with the firemen."

I raced toward my house, but felt like I was running in slow motion. A detached part of me noted that I now understood the expression about blood running cold in your veins. I knew before my eyes confirmed it that it was my house. I saw two fire engines, a ladder truck, a rescue squad truck and a fire department car. Hoses lay in the street. All the flashers gave the night an eerie cast. Some windows in my house were broken and the front door had been bashed in. I didn't see smoke, but I smelled it. I saw firemen walking toward the back of my house. Neighbors stood in nearby yards, most wearing robes or coats over pajamas.

What stopped me cold was what I didn't see. Where were Jackie and Andy?

I looked around desperately and saw two firemen returning from the back of the house—boots, coats, helmets, faces soot-streaked. I was ready to go charging up to the front door, when a hand on my shoulder restrained me.

Jerry, my next-door neighbor, said, "They're gone. Left about eight-thirty. I was reading the paper on my porch and saw them leave."

Jerry's big setter, Red, licked my hand. I slumped to the curb and sat down. Jerry sat next to me and Red licked my face. Turning to Jerry, I said, "Are you positive Jackie and Andy left?"

"Yes. She had a suitcase and a smaller bag. Looked like her dad picked them up. Doesn't he drive a black Buick? You want to use my phone to call Jackie's folks?"

Jerry helped me to my feet, led me to his house and up the front steps. His wife stood on the porch, wearing a long pink bathrobe, hair in curlers. She squeezed my arm and said, "I'm so sorry but you'll get through it. God gives us strength, eh?"

Jerry led me into the house and pointed to the phone. He went back outside as I dialed Jackie's parents. My mother-in-law answered after several rings.

"Did Dad pick up Jackie and Andy tonight?" I asked without preamble.

"Rob? Jackie called and asked her dad to come and get her and Andy. Said she needed time to sort things out. I don't know what's going on, though … No, that's for her to tell you."

Did that mean Jackie and I were separated? For an instant I felt that hollow sensation in my stomach, but then I was flooded with relief that Jackie and Andy were safe. "It's okay, Mom. Really." My voice cracked. "I'm so relieved. Oh, Mom, I'm so relieved."

"I don't understand, Rob. Are you okay?"

"I'm fine. It's just … There's been a fire. I mean, I just got back home, and the house is burning."

"What? Your house is burning? Now?"

"I was afraid Jackie and Andy were inside, but a neighbor thought he saw Dad pick them up earlier tonight."

"Oh, Rob. Oh, a fire." My mother-in-law collected herself. "Jackie's asleep. I'd better get her."

"Let her sleep. I want to find out how bad the damage is. Then I'll call back. It might be a while." I gave her Jerry's phone number so she could reach me if she needed to.

When I got back outside, Jerry said, "I already told this to the battalion chief. I couldn't get to sleep, so I took Red for a short walk and was about to go back into the house when I heard glass breaking. Sounded like it was coming from your place. I heard someone running behind your house and then a car taking off in the alley. When I saw the flames through your kitchen window, I reported the fire right away. First truck was here in a few minutes. Said they were returning from another fire."

I looked at him, not comprehending what he was saying. Then it dawned on me. "The fire was deliberately started? Who would do that?"

But, on second thought, it had to be whoever murdered the kids. Dirk or Harley seemed increasingly like the best candidate. Of course, Van Boven was out on bail. Perhaps whoever started the fire thought I knew more than I did and was trying to scare me off.

"I figured it was some neighborhood kids," said Jerry. "There's only three of us white families left on the block. I've been thinking of selling, but I hate to be part of the white exodus. Now, I don't know."

The chief approached. "You the owner of the house?" he asked.

"Yes."

"We've got it contained. It didn't spread much because all the inside doors were closed. I wish more people were smart enough to do that."

Andy and his door-closing ritual. Thank God!

The chief pushed his hat back. "Investigator's inside now. He'll be able to tell you more when he's finished. Looks like arson. Any idea who might have done this?"

I wasn't sure whether to share my suspicions, so I didn't. I shook my head.

Just then, Jerry's wife called my name and said Jackie was on the phone. I ran into Jerry's house, thankful that his wife stayed outside so I could have privacy.

Jackie's voice was tense. "Are you okay?"

"Yes, Jacks, I'm fine. I'm just so thankful you and Andy are at your folks. I mean, I'm not happy you've gone, but ..."

"I know. The house?"

"I don't know how bad the damage is yet, but the fire chief said it didn't have much chance to spread because all the inside doors were closed."

Jackie laughed. "I can't believe it. That little stinker. I got irritated with Andy when he ran around closing the doors just before we left. Do they have any idea what caused the fire?"

I told her what Jerry had reported and that the fire chief had confirmed it was arson.

"Somebody from the neighborhood wanting to force us out, you think?"

"I can't prove it, but I think whoever murdered the kids started the fire. Maybe Dirk or Harley, the guys from the gas station. Dirk may have paid Star and Cat to let him take nude photos of them before they were murdered." I told her about Sam's snooping in the upper room of the station.

"You and your detective games." Jackie's voice was flat.

I didn't respond. After a moment, I said, "Jackie, are we, um, separated or something?"

There was a moment of silence. Then, "Yes. No. I don't know. I left a note for you in the kitchen." She gave a short bark of a laugh. "I guess you didn't get it. I just need some distance." After another silence, she said, "Where are you going to stay? Do you need to come here?"

"If you need space, I'll see if I can crash with Nathan. Will you give Andy a great big hug for me in the morning and tell him he's my hero?"

"Okay. Let's talk tomorrow."

Later, after I'd heard many expressions of sympathy from neighbors, the fire investigator found me sitting on Jerry's front steps. Red sat with his head on my knee as I rubbed his neck.

"I can take you through the house now," said the investigator.

He led me through the front door, his powerful flashlight illuminating the mess. The smell of smoke was pervasive. I walked past soaked furniture, over soggy carpet, toward the back of the house. The kitchen was covered with black and gray film. The cupboard doors were charred. Some drywall had come down and the paint was blistered. To my eye, it looked beyond repair.

"It's definitely arson," said the investigator. He pointed to a broken bottle and remnants of a rag on the floor. "Pitched it in through the window in the back door. Good thing your neighbor called right away. Most of the fire damage is here in the kitchen and the smoke damage is mostly in the dining room. Damage is heaviest here where the incendiary device landed." He shined the flashlight at the hole burned in the kitchen floor. "And up here." He tilted the light toward the ceiling where the fire had burned through the bathroom floor upstairs. "Of course, there's water damage throughout the house, but the stairs are safe and the house is structurally sound. You'll have to get your insurance adjuster and their contractor in here. See where the clock stopped at two minutes after twelve." He pointed the light at the clock on the wall. "That tells us exactly when the fire started."

I followed the investigator down the basement, where everything was soaked and water covered the floor. Then we went up to the second story. Mostly water and smoke damage, a little greater damage in the bathroom.

When the fire trucks left, Jerry helped me board up the front door and those windows that had been broken. I felt disoriented as I drove to Nathan's house and rang his doorbell.

He looked surprised and sleepy-eyed. "Come in, man. What's up? You look all weirded out."

I told him about the fire and that Jackie and Andy were staying with her parents.

"You're welcome to crash on my couch," he said. "I'll get blankets."

He brought the blankets and then hustled into the kitchen, returning with a couple of beers as I called the police station and left a message for Johnson regarding the fire.

Dead bodies and fire trucks haunted my dreams.

CHAPTER 21

"**D**addy, are you coming to the farm? Can you bring me home to see the fire trucks? Will the firemen let me get inside the trucks and climb on them and wear one of their hats and everything?" Andy's words tumbled out.

I switched the phone to my other ear. "The firemen put out the fire, and then they took the trucks back to the fire station. They need to be ready in case some other family's house starts to burn."

"Oh." Disappointment in his voice.

"How about if you and I go to the fire station near my work soon so you can see some fire trucks? Would you like that?"

"Can we do it now?"

"We'll do it soon," I promised. "Did Mama tell you that the fireman said the fire wasn't too bad because you closed all the doors?"

"Yup. She says I'm your hero."

"That's right, Andy, you are. Now can I talk to Mama?"

I heard the clatter of the phone being dropped, then Jackie came on. While we didn't yet know the extent of our losses, we agreed that the only irreplaceable possessions would be photo albums, scrapbooks, and the big Dutch Bible that my grandparents had brought with them when they emigrated from the Netherlands. Jackie added her childhood diaries to the list. We hoped those treasures hadn't been damaged or destroyed.

"I'll call you again, after I get another look at the house," I said.

"Okay. I'm not ready to see it yet," said Jackie. "I can't face it. Don't forget to check on my diaries when you go. Don't even think about looking in them." We'd been at the farm one evening before we were married when she'd first shown me the diaries. "If you ever look in them," she'd said, "I'll have to take you out behind the barn and shoot you." She was probably exaggerating.

"I'll bring our treasures to the farm," I said.

"Okay. I got one of the other nurses to cover for me at work for the rest of the week."

As I hung up the phone Nathan yelled, "Breakfast!" Nathan and three of his friends, who all worked on his lawn care crew, rented the house a half dozen blocks from my place. They commiserated with me about the fire and assured me that I could stay with them as long as I needed.

Later that morning, I bought a few clothes at a department store downtown, then stopped at the religious supply store and picked up a clerical shirt. As I walked past the gas station by the Ministry I was stunned to see a sign in the window—Under New Management. A man I didn't recognize was pumping gas for a customer. I walked into the station and waited. When he entered, I introduced myself.

"How did the change in management happen so suddenly?" I asked. "Harley and Dirk never mentioned anything about it."

"We've been negotiating for the past month with the owner, and she suddenly decided to drop the asking price quite a bit."

"She? I thought Harley Scanlon owned it."

"Not that it's any of your business, but the previous owner was a woman. Harley managed it. Realtor told me Harley had to leave town on urgent family business and asked if I could start today. Sorry, but I've got a customer out there."

At the Ministry I told Lydia about the fire. She grabbed the edge of her desk with both hands. "Jackie and Andy okay?"

"They were at the farm."

"Thank goodness."

The front door opened and Johnson walked in, followed by Kincaid. "So your house got torched," said Johnson. "How bad?"

"I'm told it's not too bad, but you couldn't prove it by me."

"Wife and son okay?"

"Thankfully, they were at her parents' house."

"My contact in Detroit is convinced that both Harley and Dirk were involved in the murder of a young girl there," said Johnson. "If Boyle's got some experience with arson in Detroit, too, I bet dollars to doughnuts he did your house."

I noticed no reaction from Kincaid to Johnson's disclosure.

Lydia and I filled the detectives in on our escapade the previous night and the minimal result.

"Maybe Dirk and Harley think I'm on to them after my unintentional eavesdropping in the john," I said. "They might also figure I put Sam up to snooping in the upper room. The fire might have been started to scare me off."

Johnson glared at me. "I thought we had an understanding that you'd leave the detective work to me and Kincaid."

I'd promised nothing and now I kept my mouth shut.

Johnson sighed. "We'll interview Boyle and Scanlon again."

As he and Kincaid turned to go I said, "I'm afraid we're a step behind them, Sid." I told him about the new management at the station. "Harley and Dirk have probably left town."

"Shit! Sorry, Lydia." Johnson fingered a mole on his neck. "They've been renting a house on the West Side. I'll get someone to watch the place, and I'll try again for search warrants. Maybe the new owner at the station will let us get an evidence crew upstairs without one."

I told Johnson I was staying at Nathan's and gave him the phone number and address.

When Johnson and Kincaid left, I said to Lydia, "I noticed you didn't say anything when Johnson apologized for saying 'shit.' You could tell him that you're used to hearing a lot worse."

"Doesn't hurt to keep the man on his toes around me. And you keep your mouth shut about that, Buster."

The phone rang. "Hi, Sam," said Lydia. She filled Sam in on the latest details and then hung up. "Sam said to tell you and Jackie she's sorry about the fire and hopes everything works out."

"Okay. I think I'll take the day off. I need to connect with Jackie and see what we can salvage at the house."

The phone rang again. It was Stu Peterson. We did a brief interview about the fire.

If Dirk and Harley had left town the worst was over, I thought, as I hung up the phone.

Before leaving, I gave Lydia Jackie's parents' phone number, in case I went out there later and she needed to reach me.

As I drove to my house I thought about Harley and Dirk. I was almost convinced Dirk or the two of them were responsible for the deaths of our kids. If they had split, it probably meant an end to the murders in Grand Rapids, even if they weren't caught. The house could be repaired or we could find another. Life could get back to normal.

But how much damage had I done to my marriage by putting Jackie and Andy at risk? Jackie liked my integrity, but didn't know if she could live with it.

That hollow feeling returned.

I was too overwhelmed to do more than put one foot in front of the other. When all else failed, I had my Dutch stubbornness to keep me going.

At the house I let myself in the back door. I went upstairs to the study and opened the bottom drawer in the chest of drawers. The scrapbooks, diaries and photo albums were fine. I glanced through Jackie's scrapbook of her growing up years. While we'd both gone to Holland Christian High, we barely knew each other until I was in college and a friend set us up for a date. Yet, whenever I looked at the pictures of her as a kid, I couldn't help feeling like I'd always loved her.

The Dutch Bible on the small table was okay, too, except for a few water stains. I put everything into a suitcase.

In our bedroom I grabbed some smoky-smelling clothes, mine and Jackie's. Maybe a few washings would help. I stuffed them into another suitcase, then grabbed some of Andy's clothes. Downstairs, I gathered up the framed photos that stood on the buffet in the dining room—one of our wedding, a recent one of the family, and one of Andy swinging in the park. All were covered with smoky film. I tossed them in one of the suitcases.

Then I drove to a pay phone, popped in a dime, and called Jackie. "I'm still not ready to see the house," she said, sounding tense. "You'd better come to the farm. We need to talk."

On the drive to Borculo I prayed Dirk and Harley would be caught. When I pulled into the farmyard, Andy came running out the door. I scooped him up and gave him a hug.

"Daddy, you stink!" Andy wrinkled his nose and squirmed to get down as Jackie and her folks joined us.

Jackie said, "Andy's right. You smell like smoke. You've been in the house."

Jackie's dad carried the suitcases inside while I grabbed the clothes I'd purchased. We put everything in the bedroom that Jackie was using. She looked at the albums, the family photos, and her diaries as I laid my new clothes on the bed.

Then she said, "I'm so glad this stuff and your grandparents' Bible survived the fire. We can replace the rest if we need to. I guess we're lucky. You'd better change into some of those new clothes so I can wash what you're wearing."

While Andy played with his toys in the living room, I filled the others in on the fire and my walk through the house that morning. After lunch, Andy and I played catch in the back yard, and then I put him down for his rest. Jackie brought me a glass of iced tea and, with a glass of her own, headed for the side porch. We sat and drank our tea, looking out toward the barn and the fields.

"I know all this business with the murders and me trying to play detective has been hard on you, Jacks," I began. "I'm really sorry about that. It's no wonder you need a break to sort things through. But, damn it, it's hard on me too, and I could use your support. Now I'll shut up and listen if you're ready to talk."

Jackie swirled the ice cubes in her glass and looked at me for a long moment. "At first I was mad because you were endangering yourself which has a big effect on Andy and me. Now it appears that you are putting *our* lives at risk, too. Andy and I could have been home. That really pisses me off."

"I don't blame you for being angry."

Jackie went on as if I hadn't spoken. "This thing you've got going with Sam doesn't help either."

"There's nothing going on with me and Sam. She called Lydia this morning. She said to tell you she's sorry about the fire and hopes everything works out. You've never been threatened by my attraction to other women before. You usually just sing, 'Bring it on home to me,'" I reminded her, trying to lighten the mood.

She glared at me. "The way Sam dresses makes it different."

I laughed, and knew immediately it was a mistake. As Jackie shot me an even darker look, I said, "Look, Sam is gorgeous and has a great body. You're gorgeous and have a great body. I'm married to you, and I love you and want to be with you. And with Andy."

Jackie's look softened a smidgen. "Let me just say this." She took a sip of her tea. "I don't want you to misunderstand. I'm not saying I want a divorce. But the thing I realized last night before I called Dad to pick us up is that divorce has to be an option." Jackie plunged on before I could open my mouth. "If divorce isn't an option, then I'm stuck with you. I don't want to be stuck with you. I want to choose to stay married to you."

We'd never talked about divorce before. That familiar empty sensation was now shaded with terror. "I see your point. I don't want you to be stuck with me either, anymore than I want to feel stuck with you. But, frankly, this whole subject scares the hell out of me."

Jackie sighed deeply and her shoulders dropped.

I could see how hard this was for her. I blinked back tears.

Jackie grabbed a tissue and blew her nose. "Okay, you dumb, Dutch *dominee*. You handled this very well, but you're not off the hook yet. I still need some time. Can you stay at Nathan's?"

"Yes, the guys said I was welcome to stay as long as I need to. It's more convenient for my work, anyway, than staying here."

The phone rang and Jackie's mom yelled, "It's for you, Rob. Your mother."

I went to the kitchen and picked up the phone.

"Robbie, are you and Jackie and Andy all right? We heard about the fire from a lady in our congregation. Why didn't you call? Fortunately," she added in a scathing tone, "I learned about it before I left for Grand Rapids to take care of Andy this morning."

"Sorry, Mother. Things have been a little crazy. We're all right. Is Dad on?"

"Hi, son. You're all staying at the farm? You know you're welcome here, too."

"Thanks, Dad. Jackie and Andy are staying here. Fortunately, they were here when the fire started. I'm staying with a friend in town to be close to work and to deal with the house."

"A firebomb?" Mother's voice was even sharper than usual. "For crying out loud! I warned you about living in that awful neighborhood. You never listen to me. Could the fire be connected to the murders? It will be all over the news, and this is not the kind of publicity that will help you—"

"The important thing is we're okay, Mother. Besides, it looks like the guy or guys who murdered the kids have skipped town."

"I'm glad to hear that," said Dad.

"I've got some things to take care of. We'll be in touch with you, Mother, about taking care of Andy next week." As I hung up the phone, I told Jackie I wanted to give our insurance agent a ring to get things rolling on the house.

"I'm ready to go to the house now," she said. "I'll grab some more clothes to wash and start going through things. It just seemed too overwhelming before."

I called the insurance agent. He said he'd send someone out in the next couple of days.

Lydia called to say that Brandon had phoned to express his regrets about the fire, as had Blaine. I told her that Jackie and I were going back to the house to salvage what we could.

I glanced at Jackie who was pouring herself another glass of iced tea. With Dirk and Harley gone, a major source of the pressure on my relationship with Jackie would be relieved.

But what if they were still around?

CHAPTER 22

Jackie sat immobile behind the wheel of her mom's car. I'd gotten out of ours and was walking toward the front steps of our house when I looked over my shoulder. I came back, opened the passenger door, got in, and took Jackie's hand. Her face was pale. She stared at the house.

After a few minutes, she took a deep breath. "I feel paralyzed," she said.

"Take another deep breath and put your hand on the door handle."

She did so.

I waited another moment. "Another deep breath and then open the door."

She did, then took one more breath. "I'm ready."

We went around to the back, and I unlocked the door.

Jackie stepped across the threshold and confronted the wet, smoky-smelling mess that pretended to be our kitchen. She stood there, hands on hips, taking in the ugly scene. "So somebody tossed the firebomb through the window in the back door, and the fire started in here."

"That's right."

She stepped carefully around the hole in the floor, marched down the basement, and looked around. Then she marched back to the main floor, through the dining room, living room and upstairs. After looking in all the rooms, she turned to me. "Let's go sit on the front steps for a bit."

No sooner had we sat down than Jerry's wife hurried over with Red trailing her.

"Oh, Jackie, I feel so bad for you," she said. "It must be in the Lord's plan, though, and everything will work out for the best. He promises that, eh?"

Jackie looked at her evenly. "I know everything will work out for the best, but I don't agree that this crap is part of God's plan. This is the work of some S. O. B., and I hope they find him and lock him up for a long time."

Jerry's wife looked like a small animal caught in the headlights, but she quickly rallied. "I hope they catch him too, dear. Anything I can do to help?"

Jackie sat down again. "Not right now, but thanks. I just need to let this all soak in a little." She laughed. "No pun intended. Then Rob and I need to see what we can salvage."

Red pushed his head against Jackie's hand until she absently patted him.

"Just come over if you need anything, you guys, eh?"

Before we could let things "soak in," a motorcycle and a couple of old cars pulled up. The Lost Souls poured out and trooped onto the porch with three pizzas and a couple of six packs of pop.

"Lydia told us about the fire and that you guys were here," said Lawton.

After we chowed down with the Souls, they toured the house to see the damage, and then, once again, gathered on the porch. Jerry's wife returned with a plate of Dutch wind-mill cookies, Red in her wake. I made introductions, and she passed out cookies to a very polite and well-mannered group of scruffy-looking kids, all wearing their colors. She was most gracious, and Red soaked up attention from the gang, tail and butt wagging up a storm.

Eventually the kids left, and Jerry's wife returned to her house. "The Souls really are decent kids," said Jackie. She rubbed the back of her neck. "I've never been gang-helped before. I can see why you love them so much."

We were about to go back into the house when two other neighbors crossed the street and delivered a mess of fried chicken and a hot dish. Jackie suggested I take the food to Nathan's.

After we'd finished at the house Jackie headed back to Borculo, and I returned to Nathan's pad. He and his crew trooped in a few minutes later.

"By the time you're cleaned up, dinner will be on the table," I called from the kitchen.

Half an hour later, we were seated around the table. The guys dug into the fried chicken and hot dish with great enthusiasm. As we lingered, drinking coffee, Nathan patted his stomach. "If you keep feeding us like this, we may never let you go back to Jackie."

"Don't get your hopes up," I said. "I don't expect the neighbors' contributions to continue. Besides, Jackie's a lot cuter than any of you guys."

Nathan gave me a spare key to the house and suggested I rest while they cleaned up. I stretched out on the couch.

The sound of the phone ringing woke me. "It's Johnson," called Nathan.

"You and Lydia prowling the streets tonight?" the detective asked.

"I'm just about to leave and pick her up."

"How about stopping at the station. I'll fill you in on some things."

Half an hour later, Lydia and I sat across the desk from Johnson. Kincaid looked up from his typewriter and nodded at me.

"We found Scanlon's Chevy and Boyle's Ford pickup at Kent County Airport," Johnson said.

I felt myself relax. "So they've left town."

The big detective scowled. "Maybe they just want us to think they did."

"Did you check with airport security?" I asked, my body tense again.

"Airport security," echoed Kincaid. "Now there's a witticism worthy of note."

Johnson shot Kincaid a frown, then ploughed on. "We showed them a sketch of Scanlon and a mug shot of Boyle. Also showed the pictures to ticket agents. Nothing. No paper record of their flying out of the airport either, though they could have paid cash and used aliases."

"Did you check car rental agencies?" asked Lydia.

Sid's left eyebrow went up a notch. "Yeah. The girl at Hertz said that maybe Scanlon looked familiar from the sketch we showed her. A one-way rental to Kalamazoo. Police there are following up on it."

"Sid," I asked, "could I get pictures of Dirk and Harley to show to a few people?"

Kincaid produced copies from the inside pocket of his jacket. "You may have these. We have more."

I looked at the two grainy pictures. They would have to do. I put them in my shirt pocket.

"One more thing," said Johnson. "The new owner at the station let us get a crew upstairs. It was wiped clean. You were right about there being a two-way mirror up there with a room behind it."

I told myself that the room had probably been empty when Sam was up there, but my gut wasn't buying it.

As we walked to my car, Lydia looked worried. "Let's go to River City. We need to let Sam know about that mirror and that Detective Johnson suspects Dirk and Harley haven't left town. She could be in danger."

"I was thinking the same thing."

At River City, the bartender saw us enter. When we reached the bar, he hoisted two empty beer glasses toward us. Lydia and I nodded and he turned to fill them from the tap. Sam, who was waiting on customers near the pool table, spotted us and waved. Lydia headed toward the pool table with her beer while I stayed to answer the bartender's questions about the fire. I showed him the pictures of Dirk and Harley. After a few minutes, I took my beer and joined Lydia and Sam in a booth.

"Detective Johnson thinks maybe they haven't left town," Lydia was saying.

"I've been worrying about that mirror we talked about," said Sam.

Lydia frowned. "You have good reason to worry. The police got permission from the new owner of the station to check out the room. They confirmed that it's a two-way mirror.

"Did you tell Dirk where you worked, Sam?" I asked

"Are you kidding?"

"All the same, I'd be especially careful leaving work." I showed her the sketch of Harley.

"You two are scaring the shit out of me," she said, studying the picture.

"Good," I said. "I think it's best if we all run scared until they catch these guys."

Glancing up at the bar, Sam caught a signal from her boss and slid out of the booth to wait on customers.

When she returned, she reached across the table and took my hand. "Rob, they already torched your house. You and Jackie have to be careful."

"We all do, Sam."

Her eyes dimmed, then brightened. "Seriously, my life has gotten really interesting since I started hanging out with you two. Not that it was boring before. But, wow! Not like this. There's nothing I hate worse than boredom."

Lydia and I finished our beers and left the bar. We sat in the car for a moment, windows rolled down to let in the evening breeze. My shoulders slumped and I sighed.

"You look like you're carrying some heavy stuff, Rob."

"It's all this time and energy that we're putting into trying to help the cops catch the killers. Helping the kids cope, that's ministry. But the rest of it …"

"Perhaps helping to solve the murders of your congregation members is your calling right now. Maybe you are doing ministry when you're playing detective."

I considered Lydia's words. What she said made sense. Or was I rationalizing? I thought of Jackie, my mother. Definitely rationalizing.

I'd already endured an attempt on my life, lost my home to a fire, put my family in danger, and jeopardized my marriage. Maybe my job was at risk, too, given old John having a burr up his butt about my nosing around. Was it worth the cost? But I kept coming back to the same thought: If I wanted to feel like a decent human being, I had to pursue this wherever it took me.

I started the car and headed back downtown. I couldn't think of anything to do related to the murders, so I said, "Where do you want to go?"

"What say we go to Koinonia? There's a guy doing Arlo Guthrie and Bob Dylan music. Nathan says he's pretty good."

"Are you into Guthrie and Dylan?" I asked, surprised.

"Ever since Nathan loaned me some of his tapes."

We parked a half block from the coffee house. A couple of heads joined us on the sidewalk, and we entered together and found a table with them. The performer was doing "Blowin' In the Wind." When the musician took a break, we talked about the murders.

The conversation shifted to the Vietnam War and some of the troops coming back. I found it difficult to focus, my mind staying on the murders. I wondered where Dirk and Harley were and if I'd see them again. Why in the heck would they stick around, if indeed they had?

"You're playing with your beard again, Rob," said Lydia.

I was too agitated to sit any longer. "I'm ready to go, but if you want to stay and hear this guy, I can pick you up later."

"Yeah. Stick with us, Lydia," said one of the heads.

"What are you thinking of doing, Rob?" she asked.

"Maybe dropping by the Ministry to see what's happening."

"If that's where you're going, I wouldn't mind staying. If you want to go anywhere else, get me first."

"I'll go to Drop-in for a while. Catch you later," I said.

I could have walked from Koinonia to Drop-in, but I was feeling a little spooked. It might be better, I thought, if I took the car.

I pulled up to the traffic light at Fulton, vaguely conscious of a dark late model sedan coming toward me from the east. As it moved slowly through the green light, the driver looked at me. At the same time, the passenger pointed in my direction. I assumed the artwork on my car was attracting attention as it often did.

Then my gaze locked with Harley's. The passenger was probably Dirk. I squealed around the corner. I headed west on Fulton as Harley began a U-turn. I checked my rear view mirror. He'd been slowed by a car behind me. I was a block ahead of him. Harley passed the car between us. He rapidly closed the distance.

I hit the brakes and took a right turn on two wheels. Holy shit! That was a new sensation. I was glad I wasn't facing the weekend circuit traffic. I saw only one other car headed toward me as I sped through the heart of downtown. I ran one red light, then another. I heard a loud report and realized they were shooting at me. Then, two more shots.

As I passed the front of the Hall of Justice which housed the police station, I had a flash of jumping the curb, driving up the sidewalk and crashing straight through the front door into the lobby. Then I remembered the vehicle entrance to the station. I hit the brakes, made a hard left on Michigan, narrowly avoiding a car about to move through the intersection. I made another hard left down the ramp to the basement entrance. A young uniformed officer was getting out of his vehicle. I squealed to a stop, nudging the rear bumper of the cruiser.

"They're chasing me! They're shooting at me!" I shouted through my open window. I must have sounded hysterical. Or high.

The officer looked freaked, but collected himself quickly, one hand resting on his gun. "Step outside the car, sir."

I did as he demanded.

Other cops came running, as the young officer confronted me, his hand now touching the handcuffs on his belt.

He noticed my clerical collar. His body froze with indecision. After a moment, he looked toward the other officers for a clue about what to do next.

An older officer stepped forward. "You're Vander Laan, from the Street Ministry, right?"

"Yes," I said, still charged with the adrenaline rush.

"So what's with your unorthodox entry here, sir?"

I quickly told him what had happened.

"Did the guys who were after you make a left at Michigan too?" the older cop asked.

"I don't know. I wasn't watching my mirror anymore."

He instructed three officers standing with him to fan out from the station. "Remember these guys are armed and dangerous. Go!" He turned to the young cop whose cruiser I'd bumped as the others ran for their cars. His gaze moved down to where the young officer's hand still rested on his cuffs. "I grant you, it'd be fun to bring in the Reverend with handcuffs on, but that might not be the best idea."

The young cop dropped his hand to his side.

"Pretty smart thinking, pulling in here, Reverend," said the older officer.

"Call me Rob, please."

The older officer put a hand on my shoulder. "Come into the station, Rob, and we'll get your statement."

I walked inside on rubbery legs.

I'd finished making my statement when Johnson and Kincaid came in. I rehashed the chase with them.

"So we know they're still around," mused Johnson, rubbing his chin, "and we know they're after you. If they murdered the kids and their cover's been blown, seems like they'd disappear. What's so important about getting you? It's not logical." He scowled and shook his head.

"Perhaps it would be a good option for you to take a holiday with your family," suggested Kincaid.

I felt exhausted, but I sat up straighter. With an effort I pulled my shoulders back. "I'm not going to do that." Maybe it was just my stubbornness. My mother sometimes called me a *stijf kop*—a stiff head.

"We'll keep an eye on your car, the Ministry and Nathan's place as long as you're staying there," Johnson said. "But we can't protect you all day, every day."

"I know that, Sid."

"Wish you knew for sure what kind of car they were driving or you'd caught the license number, but I guess you were too busy getting away from them. Wouldn't be surprised if they ditch that car. Anyways, we found one bullet from a 357 Mag in your right rear tire. Surprised it didn't go flat, but that happens sometimes. One of the guys put your spare on. We'll keep the tire for evidence, but your car is all set for you."

"Don't forget to replace the spare," added Kincaid.

I left the station and picked up Lydia at Koinonia. Together we walked out to my car. "You look terrible, Rob," she said, peering at me. "What's the deal?"

"Dirk and Harley," I said.

CHAPTER 23

Surprised the guys had slipped out without my waking up, I called Jackie after a quick breakfast.

"I'm doing fine," said Jackie. "At least I haven't been shot at lately."

Had to be the dang Dutch grapevine. "How did you hear?" I asked.

"Your sister called from Rock Valley." Rock Valley was in Iowa, but distance mattered little to the grapevine. "Her neighbor has a friend in Grand Rapids whose husband is a GR cop. Anyway, I gather you're okay?" Her voice carried a note of resignation."

"I am. You want go through more stuff at the house today?"

"How about meeting me there at noon?"

"What say we meet for lunch at Woody's Restaurant and go to the house from there?"

"That'll work."

I hung up the phone and started upstairs to shower. Then I came back down, thinking I'd better call my folks before they heard via the grapevine, too.

My mother answered after the first ring. "Is Dad there, too?" I asked.

"Just a minute. I think he's coming in the back door."

At least she hadn't heard yet. I waited a moment till Dad picked up the other phone. "Son, are you okay. I just heard."

"What's going on now?" demanded my mother.

Would I ever beat the fricking grapevine?

"What'd you hear, Dad?"

"The minister at Sixth Street just called. The nephew of a man in his congregation is a Grand Rapids police officer. I guess he's the one who handcuffed you when you came flying into the police station and crashed into his cruiser after getting shot at."

"Getting … getting shot at?" Mother spluttered. "Robert Melvin Vander Laan, what is going on?"

"I wasn't handcuffed, and I didn't exactly *crash* into the cruiser." I told the story again.

"You should have called sooner," said Mother. "It's very upsetting to keep hearing about your problems from—"

"I didn't call to listen to you criticize me Mother. If you keep that up, I'll stop calling."

I imagined both ends of the phone line steaming.

As soon as I hung up, Stu Peterson from the *Times* called. We did a quick interview about Harley and Dirk chasing me through downtown.

After I showered, my insurance adjuster called to set up a meeting at the house for later that day. A little before noon, I drove to Woody's to meet Jackie. I found her in a booth, looking pale and tired. I probably looked the same.

While we waited for lunch to arrive, I showed her the pictures of Dirk and Harley that Kincaid had given me. As I repeated the story about the chase and the shooting, the color returned to her face. By the time I finished, her neck was red.

"Those arrogant jerks." Her voice was a harsh whisper. "Rob, I brought Dad's gun." She patted her purse where she apparently carried the 9 mm that her dad had brought home from the war. "I want you to carry it."

"No way! You keep it. You're a lot better with it than I am. I'd probably shoot myself in the foot or someplace worse. How would I carry it in this hot weather anyway? In your purse?"

Jackie sighed, then nodded slowly. "Why not carry my purse? You're such an unorthodox *dominee* anyway. Or we could get you a holster. And a cowboy hat." She began to giggle. "You with your clerical shirt, cowboy hat and gun."

We both lost it until other patrons began looking at us. Whenever I thought my funny bone had atrophied with age, Jackie had a way of touching it. With effort, we sobered as the waitress brought us our lunch.

The afternoon passed quickly. At the house, we gathered more clothes and bedding and loaded everything into Jackie's mom's car. The insurance adjuster went through the house, made sure we had a place to stay and said he'd get back to us. At Jackie's insistence, I parked my car in our unattached garage, which was off the alley. Much as I disliked hiding Night Watch, I agreed with Jackie that it was better not to drive it till Dirk and Harley were caught.

Jackie drove me to the airport to pick up a rental car and then headed back to Borculo. When I returned to Nathan's, the guys made me tell the story again of the chase through downtown, even though they'd heard something about it on the news already. I asked what they thought of my augmenting my usual attire with a gun and cowboy hat.

"Don't forget boots," offered Nathan. "It's time you get rid of those clunky wing tips anyway."

"They aren't clunky," I protested.

"Clunky," echoed the three housemates.

A phone call from Brandon Sharpe interrupted our wardrobe discussion. He displayed his usual curiosity for details regarding my car chase and extended his support. "I have to say," he said, "I'm stunned to hear it was Harley and—what did you say the name of that guy who works for him is?"

"Dirk."

"Yeah. I've seen him a time or two at the station. So you think they're the ones who murdered the kids and fire-bombed your house, too?"

"I'm sure of it. I just can't figure out why they risked torching my house and shooting at me last night instead of getting out of Dodge."

"Guess I was wrong about Van Boven being the killer. Let's pray Harley and Dirk left town."

Before I could return to the table, Lydia called to say a meeting was planned at River City Lounge with Sam and Lawton. "By the way," she added, "we missed you at the service for Deacon. His mom knew about the fire and your scary ride through downtown. She said to tell you she understands about you missing the funeral."

Shit. I'd completely forgotten about it.

* * *

Sam set three beers on the table where Lydia and I sat with Lawton. Sam leaned over and took my face in her hands. "Yup, alive and well." She gave me an awkward hug.

"I'll probably be in and out of this meeting," she said, "It's getting busy." She looked quickly around the bar, and then perched on the edge of the booth next to Lydia. "Tell us what happened, Rob."

I did. Each time I told the story, I found my fear diminishing.

When I finished, Sam made another quick survey of the bar. "Gotta go. I'll be back."

"Here's what I figure, Rob," said Lydia. "If you don't want to be a sitting duck, we go after Harley and Dirk. I don't know why, but they're determined to get you and are not giving up."

I wished she were wrong. Their sticking around to nail me still didn't make sense, but in my gut, I knew Lydia was right. That meant I had no choice but to go after them. "Problem is we have no idea where they are."

"That's true, but we know they're looking for you. So you have to be the bait." She put up a hand to ward off my objection. "I know. It's dangerous. But so is doing nothing. Look at what happened last night."

"Lydia's got a point, Chaplain," said Lawton.

"Hypothetically speaking, how would you proceed with this fishing expedition?" I asked, beginning to be intrigued.

The look on Lydia's face reminded me of a teacher dealing with a particularly slow student. "Night Watch, obviously. Since they're looking for you, it's a waste to hide your car in your garage."

"You wouldn't actually have to drive it," offered Lawton. Lydia and I looked at him. "If the *car* is the bait, you just have to park it where they're likely to see it."

I pondered Jackie's insistence that I keep my car hidden in the garage. She might think using Night Watch as bait was too risky. But what the heck. Dirk and Harley knew what I looked like, where I worked, where I lived. Well, used to live. What difference was a short drive in my car going to make?

"Okay," I said, warming to the suggestion. "Let's propose the idea to Johnson."

Sam slid in next to Lydia. "Fill me in, quick."

As Lydia finished bringing her up to date, I rubbed my palms together. "Now, where to park the car," I said. "I'm thinking South Division near my night ministry stops."

Lawton said, "Mad Dog went to Muskegon today, but if we wait till he gets back tonight, he and Red Feather can join us for a little added protection."

"All right," I said. "If Johnson goes for it, we'll do it."

"Let's give it a shot," said Johnson, when I called him from the pay phone at the bar. "One of our unmarked goes with you, though, or it's no deal."

"Okay, but not too close to us."

"Agreed. You ready to place your car now?"

"No," I said. "It'll be a couple of hours. I'll call to let you know when we're ready."

As I walked back to the table, Sam brushed by me without seeming to see me, a sour look on her face. Lydia said Sam was pouting because she couldn't go with us.

We told Lawton we'd see him later at the gang's apartment and left the bar. I drove to the Ministry. When I pulled up to the curb to park, Nathan came down the steps and crouched down to look in the passenger window. "Deacon's mom called. She said that some of Deacon's friends are having a gathering at her place now and you'd be welcome if you can make it. Here's the address."

When Lydia and I arrived, Deacon's mother introduced herself and led us into her crowded living room where we encountered twenty or so young people, guys and girls, some heads, mostly straights. There was a chorus of greetings from the heads, and Deacon's mom introduced us to the straights. I sat down on the floor near the door and Lydia took a seat on the couch.

We talked about Deacon, sharing things we remembered. There were tears and laughter. Someone said that Deacon had gotten his nickname because he wasn't afraid to talk about his faith. A "Jesus freak" one of the heads called him, and he said it with respect. A couple of the kids talked about what a bulldog Deacon could be when he latched on to some cause he believed in. It had gotten him into trouble more than once. That reminded me of Deacon saying that he wanted to check into something related to the murders. Had his doggedness gotten him into the ultimate trouble? The kids also talked